The Shaving of Karl Marx

For

Stovella

The Shaving of Karl Marx

An Instant Novel of Ideas,
After the Manner of Thomas Love Peacock,
in which
Lenin and H.G. Wells
Talk about the Political Meaning
of the Scientific Romances

— ■ —

Illustrated
by
Larry Kowalski

— ■ —

by

Leon Stover

THE CHIRON PRESS
Lake Forest, Illinois
1982

First Printing

ISBN 0-942506-02-2

FOREWORD

Public interest in the Minton Affair has been revived by family fears of Egon Tersoff's demise by the same dark forces he claimed, in his highly publicized defense, were the ones that caused the death of Minton himself. Tersoff claimed he was the dupe for Minton's murder, but fled the country without ever saying why.

Now we know. A collection of letters passed into our hands by his attorney, gives every indication that he is alive and well in Rebel Russia.

The letters bear a series of postmarks, which trace his flight westward from Chicago through Tokyo, across Siberia to Moscow, and thence to a place unregistered we believe to be somewhere in the Caucasus Mountains. And there they end. We publish them intact, in his queerly terse telegram style. Tersoff!

For memories in need of refreshing, Egon Tersoff is a college teacher of Russian origin, who before his trial used to hold an untenured post in history at the University of Chicago. Teachers without tenure are easy to fire.

His grandparents got out of Russia at the time of the Civil War, like many Whites fleeing the Reds, by escaping to Japan. From there, most of these refugees departed for Europe or America. A few stayed to settle in Tokyo, Yokohama and Osaka, the major commercial centers. Among them were the Tersoffs, who made their living first in trade and then as teachers of foreign languages and literature in the Japanese university system. Egon Tersoff's father taught German and Russian before taking up a position at Columbia, so as to educate his two sons in the United States. Children of professors there, as at all big American universities, get faculty scholarships if they want, that is, free tuition. After earning their degrees, Egon's brother returned to Japan to teach American literature, his field of study, while Egon himself went on to Chicago to teach his, modern Russian history.

As if his family's forced flight from the terrors of revolution were not enough, a number of his other kinsmen were liquidated under Stalin, making him quite the ugly anti-Communist. This offensive attitude slowed his career, kept him from advancing up the tenure track, the more disaffecting him. Those insensible to the evils of the Soviet regime were the fools of a "credulity cult," as he called it. And foremost among these wicked cultists in his view was his colleague in advance of him in Russian studies, a Professor Minton. Their antagonism was well known in the academic community, albeit tempered by ties of an old friendship antedating their Chicago association, but this was played down with Minton's death, and Tersoff was accused of wreaking him with whiskey poured from a poisoned pocket flask, while the two travelled home together from a trip to Moscow for an international conference held on Lenin's anniversary, the 125th anniversary, to be exact. His cup did cheer and then eliminate.

It didn't happen that way at all, the charge was falsified, though never proved to be in court. The long trial was inconclusive, cause for making public what came to be journalized as the Minton Afair. Egon Tersoff was not indicted, the trouble only began. Misused, he disappeared and went on a mysterious journey. On the way he sent letters back to his attorney trying to explain his problem and what he must do about it. His instructions were to publish the letters should he fail and die in the process. At least, he said, he would pay off his legal fees! The letters are published, they are this book. But its author is not dead, merely gone beyond return. Chapter headings have been added.

— The Editor

LETTER ONE

Concerning The Minton Affair

Lenin, 1902.   London.   He takes two rooms upstairs at 39 Holford Square.   Near the British Museum.   ·Wants to use its library, like Karl Marx before him.   Sit in the same carbuncular chair, now a museum piece in its own right.   Wants also to learn spoken English.   Puts ad in papers.   Offers Russian in exchange. Who answers but H.G. Wells!.   Lessons base on discussions of THE TIME MACHINE.   THE INVISIBLE MAN.   THE ISLAND OF DOCTOR MOREAU.   THE WAR OF THE WORLDS.   FIRST MEN IN THE MOON.   Science fiction.   Lenin eats it up.   Is more Leninist than Lenin.   Is **origin** of Leninism.

That's the start.   End is 1920.   Wells visits Lenin in the Kremlin.   Afterward, Lenin writes him a letter he never

2

receives.   Thanks him for the English lessons.   The bicycle rides along the English coast, across the Channel from Calais.   And not incidentally for the party-state idea.   The Communist State!   It doesn't come from Marx, it comes from Wells!   Some heresy! Mattered little to Lenin by then, health failing, ready for a stroke.   Letter is cry for help.   Not Lenin's only before the "conniving" Stalin (word used in **Last Testament**) poisoned him when clear stroke not fatal, would recover.   Says the shaving of Karl Marx is overdue.   His face two-thirds beard, vast inane woolly beard making normal exercise impossible.   Lenin very hep on exercise, had been from days of prison and exile.   Beard matters to J.V. Stalin, however.   Thug who takes over revolution, lacking the dialectical wit of its maker.   Has need of its Hairy Writ instead. No wonder letter snatched!   Same with **Last Testament** dictated on sick bed, asking Bukharin to be successor, Stalin to be removed from Politburo.   Never reached Twelfth Party Congress for action. Sent via Trotsky, Trotsky run out of Party, Trotsky killed in Mexico with ice pick.   Bukharin liquidated at 1930 witch trials.   Copy held by Krupskaya (Stalin failing to get her too), so we know about it.   Wells letter unsuspected.   Counted on to publish, his article written around it, like typical Wellsian manifesto, certain to feature on front page many newspapers all Western countries.   Change pressure on Russian events.   Wells the first and biggest of the big time international pundits.   Went on to visit Stalin and Franklin D. Roosevelt.   Just checking up on world affairs, offering a few cosmic suggestions.

Letter never got to post office.   That small rat with a big camera, from commissariat of Foreign Affairs.   One of Stalin's agents.   Took pictures of Messrs. Wells and Lenin in conversation.   Listening all the time.   Even shushing Lenin now and again.   Don't talk real stuff in front of outsiders.   This to Chairman of Sovnarkom in own office.   It was Minton found a carbon in the Lenin Library, one of the greats after the Library of Congress.   Found it folded inside Lenin's personal copy of RUSSIA IN THE SHADOWS, Wells account of visitation out later that year.   Much **underlined** and punctuated!!!   Approval from same reader who had set of Wells translated first thing after revolution when state publishing house ready to go.   Book has one of Mr. Rat's photos in it, the one blown up and paraded about streets of Moscow during 100th anniversary of Lenin's birth.   Lenin in the Kremlin Festival, complete with actors in Lenin make-up, like so many avatars of Santa Claus, lecturing on street corners, in factories, offices.   That's all the poor bastards have to look forward to. Endless anniversaries.   The October Revolution.   The founding of

4

the Red Army.   The beloved KGB.   The Communist Youth League.   The defeat of Germany.   The birth of Marx.   &c.

The 115th Lenin anniversary of 1985 both Minton and I attended.   He, being the naive believer, was invited to give a commemorative lecture at Moscow University.   Big deal.   How Russians love foreigners' approval.   But then again, even fellow travellers aren't to be trusted.   Lecture printed in full in PRAVDA.   Respectful writeup with many quotes in NEW YORK TIMES.   University president wires him a promotion, jumped up to full Professor.   I'm still Assistant without tenure.   The motive, so they say.   Coroner opines he died of complications from terrific flu.   Started wheezing after we changed planes at New York for return home to Chicago.   Falls out of cab almost on doorstep. Good timing.   Then mysterious "friend" shows up to collect papers in evidence of rivalry and murder.   Widow brings charges. Sensation.   Public hates academics anyway.   News of professional jealousy a heart-warming scandal.   Trouble is, papers already given to me, together with same-size shoes and suits.   While deposition is being held, autopsist hired by him finds drug-store poison, brand X.   Preposterous.   I can guess what legit forensic sleuth would find.   Under skin on leg a teeny-weeny BB hollowed out, containing residue of poison **not** brand X.   Probably fired from pellet-gun in furled umbrella, gimmick used for assassination of Hungarian dissidents in London. Just bump into victim in crowd and let timed-release ingredients go to work. Give your cold to Contac. At least am not in jail for convenient disposal later by homicidal bunkmate. Am free to go. No proof. But warning is given, or else hunt is on.

Minton's death worth it, to be sure, but not by tenure-seeking coward like me. Worth it to the KGB. The CIA. Even the goddamned oil companies. Just to keep status quo. Nobody wants new revolution. Now that U.S. buys oil from Russians. Who get it as Danegeld from Arabs. Minton died correction, was killed, end correction to keep four score Saudi sheiks in palace robes, Americans in gasoline (add Europe, Japan), and Bolshevikland happy in Marxist fantasy. Certainly worth it, maybe. Not if I'm next.

The letter I do not have. Neither did Minton ever. But **they** don't know that. It rattled him mightily. True believer that he was. Yet he didn't destroy it. Didn't put it down Memory Hole like a good comrade should. Nor did he put it back. Someone else might stumble onto it. No, he hid it someplace in the open reference shelves. Didn't say where, not trusting me that much. Just in case he decided he could make a better career as a bourgeois objectivist historian than as a proletarian bullshit historian.   Therefore, had to slip it for safekeeping in something ornamental and not looked into.   Probably COLLECTED WORKS OF LENIN.   Say vol. 36, "Correspondence, 1920-21."   The purloined letter.   Easy to remember if he wanted to go back and sneak it out.   Risky all the same.   Exit guards even read your notes.

Well, he agonized about it there in our room at the Hotel Ukraina.   Room?   The inside of a barn!   Hallways as wide as boulevards.   Stalinesque.   M O N U M E N T A L architecture.   We're old graduate school buddies, going back to students in Russian Institute at Columbia.   Always confiding his woman problems.   Now this.   Wouldn't **believe** the rooms were bugged.   I got him out of there before he could do more than recite the whole letter.   "My Dear Wells.   Thankyouthanks, heresyheresy, shaveshave.   Your friend, (signed) V.I. Lenin."   Too late to change the subject.   "Wanna see Khrushchev's grave?" "Yeah!" he said.   "You know where it is?"   He didn't know. Soviet expert.   On his side of things he wasn't **supposed** to know. Curious all the same.   The gravestone the controversial work of Ernst Neizvestny.   Controversial because too symbolical for socialist realism.   "Come'n," I said.   Late afternoon, our last day, no more meetings.　　　"Let's take a walk over to Novodyevichi Cemetery."　　The one lovely place in Moscow.　　Next to a beautiful seventeenth century monastery.　　　Chekhov's buried there. Prokofiev.　　Stalin's second wife Nadezda.　　We passed her on the way in.　　Fresh flowers.　　A dissident deed done every day.　　She had cried for him the tears of the grieved.　　"You know he killed her don't you?"　　Silence.　Khrushchev.　　Realistic head on platform in front of interwoven forms of white and black stone suggesting the struggle of good and evil in his life.　　I say it should've been all black.　　He agrees!　　The man told lies about Stalin, 22nd Party Congress 1961.　　Then he told me he'd hidden it.

　　　　My mistake.　　Best we stayed in room and let the mikes pick up everything.　　The finding, the hiding.　　Then the men with blue pips on their shoulders could do the looking.　　Tear the place apart.　　Reading room closed for inventory.　　Now I'll have to go back and find it.

　　　　Next morning.　　　American delegation buses to Sheremetyevo Airport.　　Waiting for the plane, Minton buys Baltic amber for wife.　　Russian wristwatch (!) and East German camera for self.　　A real patriot.　　Our girl guide goes with him over to counter to get honored speaker a discount.　　The usual toughie. High heels and no stockings.　　KGB, of course.　　Working for

8

Intourist. But she does a real dumb thing. Leaves her purse behind. On lounge chair next to mine. Must have had a sleepless night going over the tapes with her section chief. Cause for alarm. I shuffle luggage around, open purse, take quick look at papers inside. Orders for the day mention problem already shared with American ambassador. Big Texas oilman. Sleepless night for him, too. The moral agonbite of statecraft. Then official from State Bank in wrinkled suit comes over to collect unspent rubles and kopeks. No good outside Russia. Pay dollar ten the ruble inside, get maybe fifteen cents at Chase Manhattan. Wrinkled suit shows proletarian disdain for money-merit. Girl guide comes back, shocked to see purse, sees me busy with currency exchange, relaxes. Minton takes picture, me and her, then I of he and her. Film never came out, I'll bet.

My problem is, I am now **their** problem. **They** is both sides, actually one side against "My Dear Wells." But why Minton not disappear then and there? Me too. Because, with detente, it had to be a **joint** action. Home ground, foreign umbrellas. Rub out Minton when he gets back and get his confidant profoundly unconcerned with letter, booking **him** for the job. Me. It's already happened.

There goes my sabbatical. Correction. No sabbatical. Fired. Had planned to write a clutch of journal articles hip deep in footnotes (clutch, a noun of assemblage for eggs). Win merit badge for articles, get promotion to Associate with tenure. Collect eggs in one book with all footnotes in back, become full Professor. New mission. Find letter. Put it to rest for all concerned and save world. Then start quiet teaching career all over again. Sure.

Meanwhile, can't have murder charge hanging over Tersoff name. So here's the story. Same tedium given at deposition, only given more hasty. New installments to be forwarded as I can. If they get me, the creeps with furled umbrellas, publish what you've got to date. No use to if I'm alive. No footnotes, no credit at Academic U. Advantage is, author spared the reviews. "History prof poisons arch rival in Red Studies. Reveals all to lawyer, then vanishes."

Enough joshing about world salvation. Task is more limited. Merely saving this one personal life. Destination Tokyo.

LETTER TWO

Concerning THE TIME MACHINE (1895)

En route Tokyo, JAL.   Lenin not called Lenin when he and Wells first meet 1902.   Year after he is.   At 2nd Congress of Russian Social Democratic Labor Party.   SD members not yet renamed Commies until after revolution at 7th Party Congress 1918.   Then Party is CP.   CPSU after Soviet Union federated 1922.   Then Russia is USSR.   Another anniversary date.   Lenin is **nomen atque omen.**   Generally speaking, identity is grounded in finding out what one is not.   Lenin is not Volgin.   This equation he discovers during first English lesson.

The   future   Lenin   arrives   with   frowzy   wife Krupskaya.   He himself always neat.   Reddish beard and re-

12

maining hair around ears trimmed.   Three piece wool suit buttoned right.   Bowler hat on straight.   Not like scruffy imitation revolutionaries of today.   He Vladimir Ilyich Ulyanov.   Hereditary nobleman.   A man "from the people," according to Minton.   Well educated.   A practiced lawyer.   His only addiction, reading. Takes carload of books, novels and magazines on train to Siberian exile.   No smoke, drink, womanize.   Same like Wells, except for latter.   Both fond of cats, however.   In Vladimir Ilyich this very interesting.   Cat in Kremlin only cat ever kept by any big pantata.   Ego-boosting dogs for other dictators, immature like Hitler.   Lenin inner-directed type.   Not made nervous by feline haughtiness.   Decent and humane.   In private.   In office, rules by means of executions.   England spared its Lenin when G.B. Shaw kicks out Wells from Fabian Society.   Tried to organize it as basis for Wellsian party-state.   Twice the socialist candidate for Parliament.   Failed politician.   Sublimates hormic drive for power in writing literature of power.   Always the party theoretician, never the chairman.   Writes new Bible of Socialist World Civilization, telling true story of reality from creation to conclusion.   This is OUTLINE OF HISTORY, the evolution of cosmic forces and social trends from nebula to H.G. Wells.   In whom their destination is immanent.   "The World-State, c'est moi."

Quite the doctrinaire for Lenin to learn from.   Wells not want to advertise this, of course.   Bad news mixing with Russian radicals.   Documentary evidence is in Wells archives at University of Illinois, Urbana.   Ignored.   Researchers ransack papers for dope on sex life.   Not interested in politics.   So we get books about HGW and Rebecca West.   None about HGW and Lenin.

When Lenin arrives he is Jacob Richter, LL.D.   From St. Petersburg, card says.   Filled with crazy hope, he places ad. Three callers answer it.   Turned away.   Not one a famous British author.   Workers.   With bad accent.   Same as orators in Hyde Park.   Lenin at first tries learning the lingo from them, standing up close.   Krupskaya his wife gives us this image in her REMINISCENCES OF LENIN.   (Wells edited out, of course. Lenin learns only from Marx.)   There he is, balding head tilted up at base of soap-box laborites.   He listening hard.   Agitating for unionization they.   British bobbies confining the radical thing to zone in special place on open lawn for that.   Incomprehensible. He who had translated book by Sydney and Beatrice Webb on history of labor unions during Siberian exile.   Can't dig prole talk.

Fourth caller is HGW.   Lenin delighted.   Author of THE TIME MACHINE.   Had read that just after being jailed by Tsarist police, night of 8 December 1895, for messing about with St.

14

Petersburg Union of the Struggle for the Emancipation of the Working Class. I say, "messing about." It was the workers turned him in. The intellectual horning in on **their** union movement. So he writes a justification, THE DEVELOPMENT OF RUSSIAN CAPITALISM. Uses prison library. When finished, reads entire library to pieces. Has plenty of time for more. Sister and mother send him new publications from everywhere, all languages. Had hoped George Gissing would answer ad. Or maybe Arnold Bennett. Famous for social realism. But, TIME MACHINE is author-making first novel and HGW keen to talk about it. And learn Russian. He doesn't. Too interested in selling himself. The new Machiavelli looking for his Prince. Lenin not the only one, however, interested to listen. Just a few years later, 1906, Theodore Roosevelt invites HGW for private talk. Imagine that today! American President asking science-fiction writer about novel like TIME MACHINE. Lesson held in White House garden. Teddy of the glasses, the teeth, the strenuous pose. Knee up on lawn chair, talking over the back, one hand clutching it, other thrown out in familiar fistic gesture. He is full of pep and optimism about the future. HGW can count on him, you bet! No decadent society of Eloi and Morlocks will come about so long as **he** is chief executive.

Eloi are lewd, feeble, self-indulgent descendants of property owners.   Morlocks are descendants of workers, sinister subterranean monsters.   This is what Time Traveller finds in A.D. 802,701.

Lenin won't allow it to happen, either, now he gets the picture.   Now he learns what bothers him about the swinish European suavity of his former valentine and political teacher, Plekhanov.   Georgi Valentinovich Plekhanov.   Hah! Plekhanov!   Father of Russian Marxism!   Founder of Russian SD Party!   Social justice for the workers!   Dares call himself Volgin!   Lenin's hidden grievances now clarified as if by magic.

Volgin is conspiratorial hero in Chernyshevsky novel.   New idea of novel is, revolution is vocation of the New Man.   In memoirs by Russian revolutionaries, all say, "I became a revolutionary at the age of _____ after reading WHAT IS TO BE DONE? by Chernyshevsky."   Same with Lenin.   Reads it sixteen times during summer vacation after brother hanged for throwing bomb at Tsar Alexander III.   What is this novel that motivates brother?   That motivated Nechayev, another student before him, to plot killing of Tsar Alexander II?   Finds out.

No New Man this new Volgin.   Trade unions! Laborism!   Where is conspiracy in laborism?   Oh, we don't need secrecy now, says Volgin.   Now that the Tsar's own agents help

16

organize unions.   What kind of socialism is that?   Police

socialism!   To make Russia more European.   And why does Europe

permit unions?   Why, to head off the **real** socialism!

Main purpose of Lenin's stay in London is printing of

ISKRA on English press.   Moves it from Munich.   Where

Plekhanov, that fake Volgin, lives.   One of his co-editors.   ISKRA

("The Spark") is revolutionary newspaper smuggled into Russia.

The spark will kindle the flame.   Lenin can't write it all.   Too

bad!   Disagrees with entire staff.   Editorial policy set by

Volgin.   Volginism will be the end of Leninism, unless . . . .   But

wait!   Lenin not yet identified to himself as Lenin.   Only feels the

estrangement.   Tries to distance himself from Volgin by moving to

London.   No open break.   Not so far.   It will come.   Quite

soon.   April 1902.   In March, just before moving, issues a

pamphlet in search of his own statemnent, WHAT IS TO BE DONE?

Title is after Chernyshevsky novel.   Question is, how combine

socialism with working class movement?   Answer: reorganize

Party.   Party must **lead** movement, not follow it.   Must defeat

Tsarist police.   Take power.   Then what?   Question is not

raised.   Something missing.   A **theory** of power.   A new

dialectic.   Something not Marx-according-to-Volgin.

Leninism.   HGW is the tutor.   HGW gives it its anti-

Volginist idea and its name.   Leninism is theory of H.G. Wells.
Stems directly from him.   Not from Karl Marx.   Marxism a front,
finally thrown off.   Lenin admits this in "My Dear Wells" letter
that is my bane.

Lessons are held at Spade House.   This a handsome
new home built by HGW at Sandgate.   Near coastal town
Folkestone.   Atop cliff ninety feet above sea waters of English
Channel.   Rich author, big money from early science-fiction
novels, impressive house.   Yet can't stay put.   Chases girls, with
permission given by wife for some dumb reason.   Not love affairs,
only "passades," so O.K.   Family is obsolete institution, anyway.
Also chases after students.   Frustrated preceptor as well as sex
enthusiast.   After all, has B.S. from Normal School attached to
Royal School of Mines.   Herr Richter picked up out of want ads.

Richter makes his way by train from London and is greeted at
cliff's edge, at the top of a private outdoor elevator. First thing,
HGW dragoons him into staying over the weekend. Richter is happy
to, but he is polite enough to offer his arm for some heavy
twisting. That done, he is led up through the pergolas and lawns to
the low-hanging eves of Spade House. Soon-to-be-Lenin is quick to
notice the letter plate on the front door. It is in the shape of a

spade, as on playing cards. **"Spathe**?" he asks, knowing his Greek for a shovel for turning soil. **"Spatha** as well," replies HGW, giving the related Latin for broad sword. Sword and spade are cognate. Originally it had been heart-shaped, the architect's trademark. HGW turned it around. "Ah," says not-yet-Lenin. "Heart upside down is, uh, spade." "Revolution," says HGW. "Is it not turning things upside down?" Richter nods, but does not understand this heart and spade business.

HGW. Do you know the deities of the Hindu Trinity?

RICHTER. Vishnu, Siva, Brahma.

HGW. Righto. Vishnu the Possessor. Siva the Destroyer. Brahma the Creator. The interacting forces of the Spade House Dialectic.

RICHTER. (Points to door plate). This card mark is dialectical?

HGW. It is. Here, at any rate.

RICHTER. Your house is not — typical?

HGW. No, but it will be. Its dialectic will.

RICHTER. Others do not know it?

HGW. Not ever.

RICHTER. Then how —

HGW.   How will it prevail? A select few will know. And that few will govern mankind with it, a formula known only to themselves, of which the masses cannot make use. Power is knowing the hidden forces of reality.

RICHTER.   I can know this from you?

HGW.   That is why you are here. Start with Vishnu. She's the Possessor, the one female deity in this triad. She is Heart. She is love, sexual possession, ownership, private property. All social jealousies begin with sexual jealousy. Next, Siva. His outward sign is the spade in its destructive aspect, that of Sword. He clears the way for Brahma to create with Spade proper, when it is a shovel. Thus are Sword and Spade one instrument for dealing with Vishnu.   Socialism can be builded only when Heart is destroyed.   The builder and maker, with the first stroke of his foundation spade, uses force and opens war on the anti- builder.

Richter files this away in his tidy mind in a form that is likely to resemble the following schema:

SPADE HOUSE DIALECTIC

Heart	Sword	Spade
Vishnu	Siva	Brahma
Owning	Breaking	Making

The two retire to HGW's study. His wife is used to sudden and strange guests, and they are left alone in a white-walled room overlooking the sea, with tiled electric fireplace, armchairs, writing table and low bookshelves over which hang a row of photo portraits taken by HGW himself. Richter passing down the line, identifies all but one of them. This man with a pipe in his mouth and a wispy moustaches, Arnold Bennett. And here, Joseph Conrad with the pointy beard. This young man, Stephan Crane. Sad looking this man, who writes about poor people, he is George Gissing. This one with the devilish facial hair is G.B. Shaw, a mixed up socialist. But who is this?   The one in the flowery vest and starched collar supporting a melon-heavy face.

It is Henry James. He is not HGW's favorite friend. He argues the novel's purpose is aesthetic, not doctrinal. Later they break with each other on this issue. Yet all the portraits have a sameness in this light. They are humanistic writers, full of Heart. All former guests of HGW and failed pupils. In Herr Richter, a writer of political books, is a pupil of rare opportunity.

Richter takes a seat in one of the armchairs and gets right down to what has bothered him ever since reading THE TIME MACHINE. Busy with his revolutionary affairs, a promise to discuss it, given by telephone from Sandgate 061 the day his ad is answered, is what brings him to accept this weekend invitation. He is a gentleman in every respect, except for his monotonous filth locutions.

RICHTER.   Shit-person Morlocks, they are workers, yes? Why you make them sub-soil shit-beasts like that? Workers good class, make revolution.

HGW.   Not **these** workers.

RICHTER.   They kill and eat shit-head Eloi, don't they? Eloi look to me like shit-decadent capitalist swine, not pay attention to running factories, just take profits and live shit-life. All day bathing, dancing, making lovee-lovee.

HGW.   That's the Eloi, the effete ones. A useless, syphilitic class. You've got that right. But —

RICHTER.   Why you call them Eloi? They not men like gods. **Eloi,** same as **Elohim,** is Bible word for gods. Hebrew plural for Canannite gods. Super beings lesser than Yahweh.

HGW.   Well, they **are** men like gods. The biblical Eloi, I mean. In Old Testament usage, the Eloi is a term of royal dignity applied to Pharaoh and other kings. In one case, however, the usage is loaded, worldly potentates who style themselves gods — even though they be mortal.

> You are Eloi, sons of the Most High, all of you;
> nevertheless, you shall die like men, and fall
> like any prince.

From one of the Psalms, number 82, if I'm not mistaken. I make use of the name with the same sense of irony. My Eloi are **failed** gods, a failed ruling class.

RICHTER.   So, Morlocks eat them. Good riddance. Morlock workers take over factories, socialism begins.

HGW.   Is Marx really that fuzzy-minded? Let's cut through the whiskers. The Eloi stand for indifferent factory owners, you see that at least. A new power in the nation with their capital investments, yet they imitate the horsey life of the landed gentry, rich enough within a single generation to buy out the old hereditary elite and move into its manor houses. Their only concern for industry is to exploit it for profit, not to manage it for efficient results. An elite we must have, to be sure, but no longer one of privilege. We need a new elite given to understanding and purpose. An aristocracy of organizers. Or mankind will fail. Little to-day's Eloi care about progress and productivity. But — and here comes the point — **neither do the Morlocks!**

RICHTER. Still, Morlocks make class war on Eloi-shits.

HGW. For the wrong reason.

RICHTER. What means, wrong reason? What other?

HGW. Well, I ask you. Does the word **Morlock** itself suggest anything.

RICHTER. Moloch. Industrial Moloch burns up capitalists.

HGW. Very good, but not it.

RICHTER. Why not? Is logical. Dead Eloi dropped into burning trash pits, along with table garbage.

24

HGW.   The one's not eaten. Try again.

RICHTER.   Morlocks, Morlocks. Hmm. Mohocks!

HGW.   You mean Mohawk Indians?

RICHTER.   Yes. Only spelled M-O-H-O-C-K. In Paris there are the city ruffians, called **Apaches**. In England, as you must know, there is also one American Indian name which is a name for same such hooligans. Attack people at night. Mohocks.

HGW.   Yes, that was eighteenth century London.

RICHTER.   So?

HGW.   Interesting, but I never thought of it.

RICHTER.   But you should.

HGW.   I didn't.

RICHTER.   It is logical. They attack rich people in dark streets, just like Morlocks take Eloi at night.

HGW.   Let me give you some advice, which I know you will find hard to accept. Nevertheless, Ruskin says, "At least be sure that you go to the author to get at **his** meaning, not to find yours."

RICHTER.   Very well. Who are they?

HGW.   Do you know what miners call themselves in England?

RICHTER.   No.

HGW.   Mollocks. The Morlocks are mollocks. The word comes from the miner's term for rubbish, non-ore bearing refuse. They who wade about in the muck are mollocks. It's also a verb, to mollock, to muck up. Or to work in a way slipshod or slovenly. The resentful slacker in any industry uses it to describe what he's doing when he shirks on the job, or sabotages machinery, or goes on strike. It's what unionism leads to. What the socialist labor leader preaches, with his cant of rebellion. Spoil something, set fire to something, he says. The result is malice and civil war on the shop floor.   An underworld of under-productive workers. Pithecoid proletarians. Class-war carnivores. Morlocks! They are labor reluctant, labor destructive.

RICHTER.   Aha, Morlocks are Siva! Put sword to Eloi, kill, kill.

HGW.   Siva goes along with the Morlocks, true. But it's a case of Siva siding with Vishnu — with labor's claim to smash, shirk and strike. There's not a blessed bit of **creative** destruction in that. From the start, the labor movement has asked the worker to give of himself as little as possible. You want revolution? End **that.** Serving no ideals and no system, the Morlock union man simply mucks about.

RICHTER.   Why play good servant to bad master?

26

HGW.   Exactly my point. Labor leaders can see for themselves, in the lazy example of the owner–employer, that industrial success wins no prizes. They see only gay criminals at the top, a spectacle of pleasure.

RICHTER.   Therefore, workers are revolutionary class. They make revolution, or nobody makes revolution. That is Marx.

HGW.   Well, he's **wrong.** Imagine Morlocks coming up out of the their holes to make a world! What can the rude violence of the poor build? The Marxist program is limited to this: — Do you feel resentment? Discontent? Then bash somebody! It's Siva without Brahma. The purpose is not creating but wasting. Class-war socialism is but a stupid imitation of the downward hatred of the proprietor class. A pathetic, vindictive reversal of this other arrogance, a pathetic **upward** arrogance.

RICHTER.   Eloi are punished, get what they deserve.

HGW.   Punishment is not remedy. The Eloi deserve to be eaten, so what? They provide a permanent edible class for the Morlock carving tables. Nothing more. The Time Traveller finds this in the world of 802,701. Our industrial system wasted down to incurable conflict.

RICHTER.   But Marx —

HGW.   I have just shown what Marx will get you.

RICHTER.   Who, then . . . makes the revolution?

HGW.   A third directive force, my good man. A third directive force.   A new class of functional rulers.   That new aristocracy of purpose I spoke of.

RICHTER.   What is it? The Party? Not the people?

HGW.   A party, **the** Party, as you wish. **Ours,** I should hope. A directive force that will crush Vishnu, the possessive spirit, the indwelling deity of Eloi and Morlocks alike.   The passive property of the non-functional rich.   The holding-up power of the striker, the slacker. The Vishnu in **both** must be slain.

RICHTER.   Kill off worker class, also?

HGW.   Right you are.   We need to establish the world's work on a new basis. Conscription for direct public service. A labor force without any social face of its own.

RICHTER.   In factories, I lecture to workers. I have seen their faces. Nobility of toil shining in them.

HGW.   Help unionize them and it's mischief you'll see. Ape-faced Morlocks. You glorify social indiscipline.

RICHTER.   You talk against labor.

HGW.   Only labor as a **class**, don't you see? Labor divided by material self-interest from the state is not socialist. It is partizan and particularist.

RICHTER.   When workers take over the state —

HGW.   Nonsense. It is **they** who must be taken over. All men shall work, and a Great State shall their workshop be, its running the duty of our partymen to oversee — men of knowledge, men of steel, men of power.

Herr Richter is much agitated by this, the Wellsian argument driving him further away from his fatherly mentor, Plekhanov alias Volgin. His growing alienation he has yet to put in words. Wells articulates them for him, and creates Leninism. Not long after he drops out of ISKRA, leaves London, and starts another paper more in keeping with his new found purpose. It is VPERYOD ("Forward"). The Marxist revolution from below, as interpreted by Volgin, is now seen as a revolution from above, yet phrased in this language of the other. A tricky ideological business. The business of VPERYOD. Its editorial board, headed by Lenin, is the Party's Central Committee, the executive HQ of a shadow government of professional revolutionaries. When the time comes in 1917 they are ready, and take over in the name of Marxism. So it is recorded.

Until Lenin himself blows that cover story in "My Dear Wells," the most explosive letter in history.

The point Wells keeps hammering away at is that socialism is too important to be left to the workers. At this juncture the revolutionary movement is settled on a policy of laborism, helping them achieve demands arrived at in response to their own suffering. Wells redirects it. But Richter, his mind-set fixed in Marxism, does not easily change his views, instilled in him by Plekhanov.

Finally Wells has enough of words and goes into action. What does this Plekhanov look like? Richter pulls out a wallet photo, leans over from his armcahir, and places it on the writing table at which Wells is seated. He takes one look at it, jumps up and runs out of the room, shouting to his wife to get stuff from the costume closet. Wells, always full of fun even when he is most serious about his ideas, is in the exuberant habit of treating his guests to impersonations of famous writers, thinkers or statesmen. The right moment has come to dazzle Richter, although the effect on him is far from usual, but not surprising. He transfers his intellectual "crush" on Plekhanov to Wells. These early Russian revolutionaries were like teen-age rock concert fans, with ideologues for idols.

Wells comes back as the elegant Plekhanov, wearing a straw hat, false beard combed to a narrow point and with sweeping moustaches, wing collar and bow tie. The last touch is the bushy eyebrows pasted on. He is Volgin. Richter laughs, and goes along with the game. He plays anti-Volgin.

VOLGIN.   The editorial board of ISKRA will now come to order. I propose that we next demand of the government a legal press for our newspaper. Secrecy does not well serve our cause.

ANTI-VOLGIN.   Impossible. We must have secrecy.

VOLGIN.   Can we conceive of a secret strike? Can we conceive of secret demonstrations and petitions?

ANTI-VOLGIN.   It is impossible for a strike to be secret for the strikers taking part in it. Pfuh! But it **is** a secret to the Russian masses. The government, it takes care to hide the news of all such things. Omnipotent, irresponsible, corrupt, savage, shit-parasitic Russian government!

VOLGIN.   You seem to have great respect for what you despise. Have you a counter-autocracy in mind for our Party? Are you to be its counter-Tsar?

ANTI-VOLGIN.   How else out-smart political police? We must be trained, like them. We must prevent them from making a secret of every strike and demonstration. Also, on the sly, we help agitate this trouble.

VOLGIN.   Oh, no. We ought not do that. We have no right to interfere in **their** struggle, their economic struggle. It is they, the masses who need and want to live better, not we intellectuals. We are here only to assist them.

ANTI-VOLGIN.   Economic struggle!   Economic struggle! Is there no **political** struggle?

VOLGIN.   Socialism is the organization of the working class movement.

ANTI-VOLGIN.   Socialism is organization of professional revolutionaries. What can your part-timers do? Work by day, read ISKRA by night?

VOLGIN.   With the help of ISKRA they can do much. Demand lower fines for lateness. Safer working conditions. Shorter hours. More pay. Pensions. The right to strike for these things. Social justice. Why, we shall **eat up** the bosses with our demands! Ruin them!

ANTI-VOLGIN.   This mass movement is all you think of. You worship mass movement. You think socialism is the workers. But, they can get socialism only from outside. What do we see in Europe? We see the working class, on its own, is convinced only to form trade unions. They want only more wages. Shit-bourgeois money mentality!

VOLGIN. What you are saying is that socialism must be **beaten** into the brains of the workers.

ANTI-VOLGIN. How fight war without weapons?

VOLGIN. But we must keep our ties with the European democracies and their tradition of liberalism. It was there, in the West, under the freedom of the liberals, that socialism and the trades union movement began. It's not as if Marxism arose in **Russia**!

ANTI-VOLGIN. Give us organization of revolutionaries, and we **overturn** Russia!

VOLGIN. Dear me! A **coup d'etat**? Our Party is not for that. We must let the revolution develop in its own way. The revolution grows naturally out of worker demands. The protest activities of the labor movement itself. Reduction of the working day. Social insurance. Rise in living standards. When protest grows to revolt, then we Party leaders will take our place in the van. And there we are! Celebrating the arrival of social justice.

ANTI-VOLGIN.   Shit!   Revolution is not mass of people who wish to protest. It is a People we capture for ourselves.

VOLGIN.   What a disappointment you are to me. You seem to be saying the workers exist for the Party. Haven't I taught you, the Party exists for the workers?

ANTI-VOLGIN.   So **that's** what Volginism amounts to? My dear Wells, you have **named** the beast!

Transference takes place at this moment. Herr Richter reaches over to the table and takes back his photograph of Plekhanov. Staring at it for a moment in stunning disbelief, he then tears it down the middle and the two halves across. Votive-like, he returns the fragments.

HGW.   Volgin, derived from the river Volga, I should think. Not your river, is it? Too near democratic Europe. Volgin is the western spring of Russian Marxism. You're more eastern aren't you? Well then, an eastern river for you. One coursing through the Russian subcontinent, arising from a common source and outlook at one time, then diverging and growing increasingly apart, finally flowing in a different direction. That one, the one you are, must be the river Lena. You are Lenin.

LENIN.   Lenin! I like it!

*

DATE LINE: Tokyo, Japan

LETTER THREE

Concerning THE ISLAND OF DOCTOR MOREAU (1896)

Met by older brother at Narita Airport. Another academic. Father also. The family disease. Brother teaches English at Tokyo University. Full Professor. Way ahead of me. Plan is, use his passport. Enter Russia through back door. He married to Japanese lady. Very high class. Family insists he take their name. Japanese and **gaijin** living in Japan all the time go to Russia. Same way, through Siberia. On business trips. For scientific meetings. And so on. Take Russian passenger ship from Yokohama. Sail to Nadhodka. Port city just south of Vladivostok. From Nadhodka take Trans-Siberian railway train to Khabarovsk. Then Aeroflot plane to Moscow. No problem with passport not in Tersoff name. To look like brother, just let hair grow longer, put on glasses, sprout goatee.

Brother very helpful.   Understands problem.   If I not return, he ready to take heat from **Gaimusho,** Japanese foreign Ministry, for loss of passport.   For now, I rest, grow hair.   First night, takes me to movie sponsored by science-fiction fans. Students at Tokyo University mad for American SF.   They form **Uchujin** Club.   Meaning is, "Cosmic Kidney."   Don't ask me why.   Movie is Americanized version of THE ISLAND OF DOCTOR MOREAU.   Starring Burt Lancaster.   Evil genius out to control evolution.   Film is not like the novel.   Not like **any** book.   People in and out of room, noisy, door-cracks of light flashing on screen. Film runs off sproket holes, breaks.   When turned back on, hole burnt in start-up frame.   Once, twice.   Three times!   Amateur operator.   A fragile medium.   Yet Lenin keen on film as means of propaganda.   "The cinema is our most important art form," he says.   To-day, state-controlled TV.   Trick of mass communication is to get mass response.   Each individual to yield to same stimulus.   But what **is** the stimulus?   The medium?   The message?   The audience?   Not so easy to say.   No wonder police needed to back up propaganda.

After movie, **Uchujin** Club leader gets up for speech.   Talks about mad scientist tradition in SF.   Starts with

38

Mary Shelley's FRANKENSTEIN.   Ends with ISLAND OF DR. MOREAU.   HGW would not approve.

When the lesson on THE TIME MACHINE is over, HGW and Lenin bicycle three miles from Sandgate to Folkestone, stopping along the way at a small public house. Lenin remarks that it must be like the one in the village of Iping where the Invisible Man lodges, the Coach & Horses Inn, run by a Mr. and Mrs. Hall. There was a problem about the rent, and then the Invisible Man broke their windows, isn't that so?   He goes on rampaging elsewhere, robbing and killing. Lenin thinks HGW gives a bad name to science with "crazy shits" like him.   And Dr. Moreau, the same.   This bad impression is given by having both the Invisible Man and Doctor Moreau killed in horrible ways as a punishment for **hubris,** the sin of overreaching. Science is a force for good, and should not be shown to be a force for evil in violating nature. These novels should have experiments done for a more social purpose, Lenin says, and not follow the mad example of Dr. Frankenstein.

HGW.   You, and everybody else, have got it all wrong about Dr. Frankenstein.   No mad scientist, he.   Don't you remember? The monster threatens to choke him to death unless he makes for him a bride. The good doctor starts work on her, then

39

reflects on the awful offspring she will bear. A race of misbegottens to pollute the world. So he destroys her. Sane enough, Dr. Frankenstein is quite civic minded.

LENIN. Sold! I remember. You are right. And Dr. Moreau?

THE ISLAND OF DR. MOREAU, the second Wells novel of science fiction, is published in 1896. Lenin is still in the St. Petersburg prison that year when he reads it. In a way, it encourages him to keep at his practical gymnastics. He does his push-ups. One must be fit for the revolution. Can't cure sick society with unwell doctor. It's a question of social physiology. The social tissue has its pathology too, gall stones and other wasteful secretions. A useful medical metaphor suggested by Moreau for all his madness, operating without a chloroform anesthetic. He is, after all, a master physiologist whose specialty is morbid growths. And is not the body politic unwell, infected by a capitalist tumor? Capitalism is a public health problem. Let the proletary revolt, says Marx, and all will be free of disease. Nobody greedy, a wholesome utopia of cleanliness will result. But social sanitation, like any other public health measure, calls for drainage officers. Streets and wells do not clear themselves of filth and cholera. Undesirable types will have to be eliminated by force, granted. Yet HGW shows the Marxist cure to be part of the problem, the working class another morbid growth. There is no revolutionary class, only a third directive force of doctors. Can it be only the doctors are well, the partymen?

This vexing question is on Lenin's mind when he and HGW stop at the pub for a beer. They sit there, sipping . . . sipping is the word, neither man a drinker. Wells is diabetic, Lenin a plain Puritan, one who seeks no personal gain other than in power terms. He sees that Moreau can elevate animals to a sort of men, and wonders how to raise a People from subhuman Morlocks. For the Party to do so and lead them to a worker's revolution, he likewise will have to mock the divine Creator. No blasphemy for an atheist, just that morbific causes are more epidemic than he or Marx ever thought.

LENIN.   Does Moreau think he is God? He carves out beast men in vivisection room, teaches them Law. Soon as bloody bandages are off, they **break** Law. Then he strikes them with whip, his own creatures. Law gives beast people to hesitate, but does not **stop** shit-beast behavior.

HGW.   Some say God thinks he's Moreau.

41

LENIN.   Not funny.   Scalpel and whip are contradictory.

HGW.   A bad joke, to be sure. Actually, Moreau aims to **improve** on creation. This is indicated by the island's location.

LENIN.   Its coordinates are latitude 5° South, longitude 105° West.

HGW.   You have a good memory.

LENIN.   I looked it up in prison atlas. There is no island there.

HGW.   No, but one could be, if a volcanic mountain along the East Pacific Ridge pushed up from under water a little further.   You can see where this would place it . . . Just off the coast of Equador.

LENIN.   So?

HGW.   Why, near the Galapagos Islands! Formed the same way. Darwin visited in 1835, during the voyage of the **Beagle,** and there found decisive evidence for his theory of evolution. Now we know how Nature works. It is totally unreliable. Of all the animals that are born, only a few survive. And it is owing to this law of selection that evolution takes place. Nature is a reckless coupler, and she slays. The law of **murder** is the law of Nature. Our mother Nature. Her handiwork is chance, waste and pain. Life is one long tragedy, creation one great crime.

LENIN.   What difference?   Evolution is just new scientific name of God.

HGW.   Don't be silly. Do you suppose Darwin simply gave over cosmic planning, or rather the lack of it, to some other futile more anonymous agency? Moreau knows full well the horrible truth. The mutual cruelties of animals, the random murder — that is not **his** way, Nature's criminal, non-directional way. Evolution might lead **anywhere**, to the liver fluke as well as to man. We can go forward or we can go back. Moreau means to take control, and save mankind.

LENIN.   Well, his way **is** the same, pain and death.

HGW.   So it must be. Remorseless as Nature he is to study and reform Nature. Haven't you got the Dialectic by now? In Moreau's tissue work, "there is building up as well as breaking down and changing." His words.

LENIN.   I got. **Destruam et aedificabo.** Proudhon.

HGW.   Sword and Spade exactly. "I will destroy and I will rebuild." Cleanse with Siva, create with Brahma. Demodel and remodel. There is no plan in Nature, but there must be in any **made** society.   Everything will be designed.   The difference between Nature and socialism is the difference between the aimless torture

43

of creation, and the power to substitute aim for that aimlessness. Socialism will abolish chance and the waste of Nature.

LENIN.   And the pain?   Chance, waste **and** pain. What of that?

HGW.   Let us clear our minds of humanitarian cant, the notion that escape from pain and suffering is the proper object of life. The gain with artificial conduct is this: — a natural process cruel and **arbitrary** is taken over by a planning process cruel and **purposeful.** Else we are back to the crude election of the fit by a roll of the Darwinian dice. Amoral slaying, without benefit of policy and direction.

LENIN.   Elimination for cause is better, very well. But human society is not **wild** Nature. It is political.

HGW.   Quite right. Bad lives are the fault of weak statecraft. Democracy provides a low grade of security even for the unsuccessful mass, the dull unkilled. The Morlock underclass that works too little — permitted by an Eloi overclass that **governs** too little. This world and its future is not for either of them, feeble slackers and selfish. At base, human nature is Vishnu's predatory delight, the evil spirit of unearned survival.

LENIN.   Does he make make any of your directive supermen?   His creatures, they are hybrid things, mixed with animals.

HGW.   He himself is Overman, the first of a coming line of intelligent agents **exterior** to Nature. That is evident in the symbolism of his name.

LENIN.   Moreau?   What means Moreau?   Just a moniker.

HGW.   His namesake is Gustave Moreau. The French painter who does creatures half man, half beast, the Sphinx, the Gryphon, the Minotaur.   His pictures play on the duality of human nature, the conflict between passion and intellect.   Doctor Moreau makes creatures very like these, his Ape Man, Tiger Man, Fox Woman, and others.

LENIN.   In Paris, I have seen his "Oedipus and the Sphinx." A painting success of scandal. Not like in Greek classics, where sphinx-female has meeting with Oedipus, they stuggle only by means of reason, the word of the riddle. But in Moreau painting, she is, ah, very sexual, tries to make seduction of Oedipus with her jutting forward naked breasts, embracing his body, tearing at him with her lion claws.   The painting is to show how dangerous is the pleasure of the physical senses, to fight with idealism of the mind.

45

HGW.   And where else have you seen her? In my works for example?

LENIN.   So! On cover of TIME MACHINE, a picture of her. And also inside, when Time Traveller lands in future, he falls off machine at bottom of huge statue, it is a Sphinx.

HGW.   The Sphinx of Sin. The fatal sin of sexual entanglement, the Heart of all social jealousy, stronger than politics, and the cause of Eloi decadence. If Doctor Moreau is to save mankind, he must burn out this animality.

LENIN.   Yet, bad wants come back all the same. Animal passions not cured by surgery. Burning bath of pain does not make rational creatures like Doctor Moreau wants to make. What good, then, his Law? The Law of Moreau and his whip.

HGW.   You come back to that, do you? So it's the Law that troubles you. Well, let's go over it.

Not to go on all-Fours; **that** is the Law.

Are we not Men?

Not to eat Flesh or Fish; **that** is the Law

Are we not Men?

Not to claw Bark of Trees; **that** is the Law.

Are we not Men?

Not to chase other Men; **that** is the Law.

Are we not Men?

LENIN.   Rules of capitalist jungle! Yet beast folk **do** claw bark, kill rabbits, taste blood, chase each other.   Then get whipped for it.   Island is joke imitation of shit-bourgeois society.   Or what is the judge, the debt-collector or the hangman for?

HGW.   But who is it that **says** the Law?   Is it Moreau?

LENIN.   Why, no.   It is the Sayer of the Law, one of your beastly half-shits.

HGW.   Yes, and where did the Sayer get it from?

LENIN.   From Moreau, of course.   To make up for bad results.

HGW.   Wrong.   The Law is not **his** at all, although his whip has to enforce it, now it has taken hold on the island, unbidden by him.   It was his Kanaka servants who introduced this Law, mooting his experiments from the start.   No need of the whip were there a sufficient bath of pain, but for the Kanaka missionaries and their idiotic propagation of yet one more version of the Ten Commandments for the natural man.   Man collective will never please to do evil, no longer misguided from inside by a lot of complicated agonizing.   Is it any wonder the beast folk rebel and murder Moreau?   By the time he drives the Kanakas off his island it

47

is too late. He is left holding the whip for **their** cause, the place already contaminated by Kananka humanitarianism.

LENIN.   Kanakas? Kanaka missionaries?

HGW.   I thought the novel made that clear. They come from Hawaii, its native people. In the Hawaiian language they call themselves **kanaka.** The word means **man,** humankind in the obsolete sense.   Brought over by Moreau on the vomit ship **Ipecacuana,** with a load of laboratory animals.   The emitic reference, I thought, gave my feelings about them.

LENIN.   So! Punishment is on account of them. **They** teach Law, Moreau has to use whip; otherwise knife cutting in House of Pain does the job.

HGW.   Right. That burning bath of surgical pain was meant to be the cure, **therapeutic** vivisection. You will note that is why Moreau does not use chloroform — on the animals. Only on himself, so to speak. In his island retreat, he is away from the civilized world of "conscience." How cure with pain if hounded to feel sympathetic pain?   Alone, he can afford to see his dripping, screaming patients not as fellow creatures, but as a problem, a problem in the higher ethics of cruel rationality. He is harsh, but not fitful. He is pitilessly benevolent. In his House of Pain he applies the new inhumane humanitarianism that will end forever

48

those fear-restrained desires fretted under the whip. Put an end to punishments and the painful conflict between arbitrary Law and animal instinct. **The pain to end pain.** Or we shall see Nature surging up through the beast men of this planet, and presently the relapse to animality of the islanders will be played over again on a larger scale.

Lenin sits in silence for a moment, then gets up and goes over to the other side of the room where the early crowd of afternoon guzzlers are already at their dart game. He politely asks a workman for one of the darts thay are playing with, and comes back to the table, sits down and begins to examine his inner thigh. The two of them are wearing shorts for their bicycle ride, HGW providing for his guest. Then Lenin pinches a fold of skin and pushes the dart all the way through.

"Like this?" he asks. "No pain. The **only** way to get no pain, where it doesn't hurt. Moreau does foolish experiment."

By this time the workers have gathered around, joined by the publican.

"Gar!" says one of them. "The marn's gone and punkshooated hisself. Snow blood, though. Do it hurt?"

Lenin just smiles, revolves his leg for all to see. "No," says HGW, answering for him. "No pain. Just a bit of entertainment done by the old Hindu fakirs. You see, the skin down there on your thigh has very few nerve endings, widely scattered here and there — you can do the same trick — and muscles, of course, under the skin feel no pain at all."

Appreciative murmuring for the kindly explanation given by one of the local gentry.

"Am't you our Mr. Wells, though?" asks another.

"Yers, that is he," says the publican.

"The very same Mr. Wells wot broke the bank at Monte Carlo. It was the ace of spades done the trick. And that's why 'is 'ouse be Spade 'Ouse."

Lenin pulls out the dart, wipes it with his handkerchief, and hands it to the nearest workman, who then passes it reverently with two hands to the publican.

"Oo, we can't be using **this** one now."

The publican retires behind the bar and prepares a display among the local soccer trophies, while his lucky customers get a chance to shake hands with the Man Who Broke the Bank at Monte Carlo, before drifting back to their own small beer.

"Nice to meet you, Mr. Wells."

"A real pleasure, Mr. Wells, I'm sure."

"So good of you Mr. Wells, thank you."

Finally the workingmen resume their game of darts, wagering for their drinks now in hushed tones of respect for the really **big** money in the room.

"It's another Wells from Folkestone," says HGW. "They've got us confused."

"Morlocks!" Lenin says, the future chairman upstaged by the party theoretician.

HGW. But listen, you're missing the point.

LENIN. Yes! It's over there (indicates dart on display).

HGW. Well, your English is good enough, anyway.

LENIN. I show you my point. Pain is not ended where hurt is not. Now, you yours.

HGW. Very Well. When I say the pain-to-end-pain, I actually refer to a big one to consume a little one. Inverted homeopathy.

LENIN. Homeopathy?

HGW. Homeopathic medicine. To treat a disease by giving small doses of a remedy that, in a healthy person, would produce more symptoms of the disease treated.

LENIN. False medicine.

HGW. Quackery, perhaps. But not Moreau's **inverted** homeopathy. The big thing to cure the little thing. Let's go back to that other chant the beast folk recite, not the one about the Law taught them by the Kanakas, but the one about Moreau himself. Their own tribute to him and his work.

> **His** is the House of Pain.
> **His** is the hand that makes.
> **His** is the hand that wounds.
> **His** is the hand that heals.

See what you missed? Moreau is both Brahma the maker and Siva the wounder. **Wounding heals.** With the Dialectic, scalpel and spade are one.

LENIN. So? End result is more pain, not less.

HGW. What else? Pain enough to burn up harmful instincts. **Shock** therapy. What would you have? The same outworn Law of the Kanakas and the limited ethics of self-restraint? Men are not to be trusted alone in the dark. Nature did not make them for moral self-action. The want of proportion between impulse and control is too great. Look where this led the island, and the world is next, passions of the body swamping reason, and mankind dying down to degradation. What hope is there **ever** in letting humans act as they choose, providing only — only! — that they choose not to be as selfish and unsocial? They require a rational master, like Doctor Moreau and the new class of saving partymen he anticipates. Plato said it:

> He who is ill ought to wait at the physician's door, and every man who needs to be ruled at the door of him who can rule.

Self-control under threat of the whip is asking too much of self-reliance to be truly social. A truce is all you'll get, never alliance. Always there is that little, raw, bleeding, inflamed pin-point of **self**, lashed raw in the eternal conflict between instinct and mock-

53

morality.   That is the **little** pain, never extinguished, always inflamed. Would you have that forever and again, and a final day of extinction?   Or better, the **big** pain to swallow the little one? The successful cruelty of intelligent purpose — good, scientifically caused pain. Better it is to suffer for a collective purpose than for none. The House of Pain is our Ministry of Health.

LENIN.   Our SD Party — you are not a member — has different idea.   Man-making of your Moreau is one-dimensional, healthy animal side put down all the way. In your dialectical idea, less human is more.

HGW.   Well said. Less human, more social.

LENIN.   We say, change society; not man.   Make perfect society fit for men and women to live in.

HGW.   A Volginist you are, to see people through to their desires. I, too, speak of perfection, but not of **self**-perfection — the impossible ground of the old moral culture, dooming all social reform.   Living's just material.   Socialism can be won only if plenitude for humanity is taken as an objective aim, that is, one apart from the well-being of individuals. Your utopia is not **vivid** enough, it fancies the reduction of human experience to a common good. A common basis for the individual to enjoy his ease in childish

54

Eloi hedonism. It cannot be. For one, pleasure is milk and honey, for another, strawberry jam. Or goat's milk, palm wine, durian fruit, or even witchetty grubs. There is no good thing one and pleasant that all may experience in their individual lives; perfection is for the human aggregate, or there is none. The only basis for common experience must reduce to the universal nightmare terrors of Hell — fear, pain, fatigue, weakness, hunger, thirst, being bound, tortured, being battered night and day. One appeal and one appeal alone can sway utopia, mankind's most shared and least personal reaction to the **stimulus intolerable.** The common basis of the unbearable is the perfection of Collective Man. A perfect fusion of interests there will be, a perfect sympathy of feeling. Not "Forty feeding as one" under our Government of Pain, but forty writhing as one. The more pain, the more to share.

After this, the two bicycle on to Folkestone and, overlooking the harbor, silently watch the ships set out to sea, the Continent and the world.

DATE LINE: Nadhodka, U.S.S.R.

LETTER FOUR

Concerning THE INVISIBLE MAN

Siberia. Vastly open place of floody rivers. In summer. Like now, humid hot. In winter, that's Siberia! Eastern port I come to. Nadhodka. Inland from here Lenin exiled 10 February 1897. Shushenskoya on the Yenisei. Small village, three years. In first batch of books from home is INVISIBLE MAN. Related story about madman exile in hick village, Sussex. Like Doctor Moreau, cast out for unlawful vivisecection work. How the English love their pets! This in-coming stuff by mail on top of freight car loadful Lenin brings by rail and sleigh. Freeze time reading. Elsewhen, politics! Lecture to peasants. Subvert warders in district town — rural policemen, easy. Travel to meet with isolated fellow radicals. Next March, attend First Congress

57

of Russian SD Labor Party in Minsk.   Volgin again.   No!   Volgin initially.   Lenin's Marxist valentine at first sight, Party founder, Party chairman.   This is birth of Russian Communism.   Thanks to Wells, it does not remain Volginist.   Wells always most interesting writer.   Book packages opened, his latest looked for.   Science fiction.   Not kid stuff!   Ideas in it.   **Political** fiction.   End result, Lenin applies SF to government.

Nadhodka keeps funny time.   I think at first.   But, is like everywhere else in Russia.   Ship arrives from Yokohama mid-afternoon.   Is 3 or 4 p.m.   Sun tells me.   Public clock tells me, 12 midnight.   Moscow time.   When Tsar orders Trans-Siberian to be built, palace clock is railroad clock.   Across the map, day and night.   In America, transcontinental railroad goes the same. Train time not change.   Confusing for passengers.   So, railroad companies in 1883 devise time zones.   These in 1918 adopted by nation at large.   Freedom and capitalism.   No time zones in Russia.   Autocracy.   Govenment builds railroad, extends government time with it.   You know where control center is. Timetable not for passenger ease.   Same today, like under Tsar. Moscow time is Moscow authority.   Ruler is ruler of time.   Your schedule is government schedule.   Difference to-day is, what is on the schedule.   Not just rail travel.   Your whole life.

I wander in streets of Nadhodka. Waiting for train after getting off ship. Interesting town. Small port south of Vladivostock, which is closed. Far eastern military, naval, submarine base. Nadhodka only partly secret. Japanese travellers on way to Moscow must debark someplace. What I see is open to all through goers. Downtown — I was about to say in business center. I mean, political center. Area is just a few blocks, yet built heavy and squat. Monumental squares even here. Message is, your state bulks big and strong. You are small and weak. All you hear in main street is muffled footfalls of passersby. Eerie. Same in backstreets where old Siberian shanty houses are. Rustic, but not rural. No sounds of natural life. No dogs barking. No children crying. No husband and wife shouting. No radios playing. **Silencia.** Terror works.

Train moves out on way to Khabarovsk. Where I take plane for Moscow. So far I am just one more tourist, businessman or academic from Japan. Brother's passport not suspect. However, I am given compartment to myself. Intourist official next door. Other passengers, all Japanese, four to the **mesto.** Westerner is watched. On general principles, I guess.

Anyway, train is rolling along on wide-gauge Russian tracks. Alone with four beds. Long trip. I think about going to Lenin Library. Find letter. Then what? **If** I find it. Worry later. For now, I tell about kitchen breakfast Lenin has with HGW and Jane. Jane is wife of HGW. Not her real name. Just called that. Her job, type the books. Raise child. Run servants. See to the master's house guests. She, the undisturbing accessory. He hopes.

JANE.   I'm the original invisible person, you know. Not really. Stella was, wasn't she, Mr. Herbert G. Wells?

LENIN.   Herbert G.? What is "G" for?

JANE.   Didn't he tell you? God.

HGW.   Stella it is, yes, my dear. But you ought not give away my sources. She's the heroine in a novel — her name is the title — by some guy I read in college.

JANE.   Some guy you read in college! Why it's **Hinton.** Charles C. Hinton, the famous Oxford mathemetician who popularized the Fourth Dimension. You can guess where God got his idea for a time machine. Stella has a point of view really alien.

HGW.   Her scientist father experiments with her, reducing her refractive index to that of air. Makes her invisible. But she wants to stay that way.

JANE.   The strange thing about her, isn't it? Herbert G.'s **man** wants to come back, but he loses the formula and so holes up in Iping with his bottles and tries to figure it out again.

HGW.   You're forgetting that Griffin was actually **driven** out of London by people in the Establishment who to this day fear new ideas. No wonder I never got elected Fellow of the Royal Society.

JANE.   People in the Establishment! Mainly his landlady, so he burns her place down because he can't pay the rent — God's lower class background showing up in this character.

HGW.   Stella! Disappear yourself instantly!

JANE.   And the police, who are after him for cutting up cats and dogs.

HGW.   That damn dumb Cruelty to Animals Act. Did I say cats?

JANE.   Yes, and you don't get to be F.R.S. for doing **fictional** science.

HGW.   I get reviewed in NATURE magazine, don't I? Besides, Griffin merely wanted to **control** the process. What's wrong with that?

JANE.   Only a power hungry fanatic **would.** But Stella — she despairs of me and mine. "Being is being for others," she says. Just like poor Jane. She is not to fall into a self-serving concern with her own visible appearance. Altruism is all.

HGW.   My dear, we agreed —

JANE.   Yes, dear. You just go on being God. The very best teacher for you, Herr Richter.

LENIN.   It's Lenin now.

JANE.   So he's given you a new name, too, has he? I thought all the Naming of the Beasts was done by Adam. Or does the Creator play the part of His creation, as well?

HGW.   The **New** Adam, my dear, the New Adam. The old one is dead, as he was for St. Paul in his new vision of things. No less than in Dr. Moreau, he is active in Griffin.

LENIN.   Don't tell me **he** is no lunatic! After what he did? Breaks windows of Coach & Horses just because Halls asks him for rent.

JANE.   Rent, again. How cheap.

HGW.   He **had** the money. Soon enough, at any rate.

LENIN.   Yes, after he takes off clothes, takes off goggles from mobbled head —

HGW.   Oh wow! "Mobbled head," very good. The gauze wrappings — quite literary your English. Do you need me?

LENIN.   "Mobbled queen," HAMLET. Takes off everything, goes out into night, steals cash from local vicarage.

HGW.   What's to object in that? Are we not duty bound to destroy the Church and all such out-worn institutions? What's a little robbery?

LENIN.   Well, he's angry, not principled.

HGW.   And you think anger unto hatred is not a great corrective?

LENIN.   What does he correct? I see only killing and destruction.

HGW.   **Creative** destruction. Griffin's as high-minded as can be. Combining the work of Siva and Brahma, he is a smasher of Vishnu's old morality, and a bringer of the new. Faithful to the Dialectic, he's a **sacred** lunatic, a holy terror.

JANE.   His coming can't be a day too soon if liberation from altruism is what he aims at.

63

HGW.   Don't be too sure about that, my dear, if it's your own soul you insist on keeping. The days after to-morrow will see nothing of benevolence, good will **or** altruism. Private virtue is not wanted, but public service.   Not self-sacrifice, but self-abnegation. The last grief of personality washed away. Remember: — "the corner stone of Socialism is the great principle of the merging of the individual in the State."

JANE.   End quote, Herbert G. Wells, boy socialist, Friday, October 8th, 1866, National School of Science and Royal School of Mines Debating Society, in defense of "Democratic Socialism," abstracted in the SCIENCE SCHOOLS JOURNAL, founded by Herbert G. Wells, edited by Herbert G. Wells, written by —

LENIN.   Social Democracy? In '86? Before Volgin? Before me?

JANE.   That's God for you, as precocious as ever. And at that time you were where, Herr Richter?

LENIN.   Not yet enter Kazan University until next year, in '87. My dear Wells, at age 20! When I was only 14.

JANE.   He's grown up now, all of 36, family, house, full of punditry — and hasn't changed a **bit**. I suppose by social democracy you mean what he does by it, something to **replace** democracy.

HGW.   But just look where the failure of his Reign of Terror got the world of 802,701. For the want of Griffin and his kind, we get a world of Eloi and Morlocks, winding down to conflict and decay. A world wreck for nothing. Destruction wide of vision and control. On this my Time Traveller broods, sitting there in that old rusted armchair.

JANE.   Let him sit there and twitch all he wants. I don't much worry that much ahead. I live in the here and now.

LENIN.   Rusty chair in TIME MACHINE . . . Is funny kind of chair, I remember.

HGW.   Yes, you might say that. You know the symbolism of it?

LENIN.   Let me think. On top of grassy hill, Time Traveller comes upon mossy chair of corroded metal —

HGW.   " — its arm rests cast and filed into the resemblance of griffins' heads." Get it? Heads of the griffin, that chimera after which the Invisible Man is named. Spell it G-R-Y-P-H-O-N and you'll see. Gryphons never flew in this present-day world and that's why the far future goes wrong.

LENIN.   Ah, gryphon! In Greek mythology is monster having —

HGW.   But a **nice** monster.

LENIN.   — having head and wings of eagle, body of lion, goes after robbers who want to steal gold and gems of Scythia. Robbers come, gryphons fly down on them, tear them to pieces.

HGW.   Thus chastising human greed and avarice, a nice monster, as I said, much needed to-day.

LENIN.   Invisible Man does gryphon work. Not mad because he does that, eh? It he **does**.

HGW.   He does. You remember that scene, one morning before opening hours at the Coach & Horses? The Halls go down into the cellar, and I, the narrator say "Their business there was of a private nature, and had something to do with the specific gravity of beer." That's capitalism for you. **Caveat emptor.**

JANE.   In other words, they water the beer. The adulteration of food and drink done in this country is a national disgrace. What our public houses need is tough regulation.

HGW.   More   than   new   laws,   my   dear. Nationalization.

66

LENIN.   Socialize beer? Happy workers not need drink.

HGW.   Anyway, Griffin passes the cellar door just as Mrs. Hall is reaching for the tell-tale bottle of sarsaparilla parked there. Sarsaparilla hides watered beer's loss of tang and color. With his gloved finger, Griffin points at it and says, in his harsh minatory voice, "Look there!" A foreboding of the socialist motto, **caveat vendor.**

LENIN.   A fine motto. "Seller beware." Comes the revolution, we will invite the capitalists. Are you for us or against us? If they say for us, they shall work for us. If they are against us, we say, to the wall with you. We shoot them.

JANE.   Well, Herr Richter, you will just be penalizing people for having the courage of their convictions. You will encourage nothing but hypocrisy.

LENIN.   Krupskaya, my wife, the same she says exactly. She must stick to her cooking and sewing.

JANE.   So, the great revolutionist is for sex equality as well?

LENIN.   Her food is not so edible, like yours. And, I need a tailor for this (flicks dangling button on his coat, torn loose during yesterday's bicycle ride).

JANE.   The cook of all servants can't be too good for an important socialist home like ours.

HGW.   Don't mind her, **she** made the breakfast. Jessie's on holiday this weekend.   Besides, I troubled myself in designing Spade House to make things **easy** for the servants. No up and down the stairs with food and dirty dishes. The kitchen's right up here on the same floor, as you can see, next to the dining room. That's progress. You won't find that in Dr. Kemp's house for all his degrees and honors. Some phoney, him and his F.R.S.

JANE.   Sour grapes. You think you deserve a medal for one year of biology under T.H. Huxley on a poverty scholarship? He never ever **spoke** to you.

HGW.   But Kemp is not a **real** scientist as . . . as Griffin is. Look, he keeps his help in the basement like all the other aristocratic clods he imitates. A medical doctor he is, and does he live on his practice? No. He dabbles. Does amateur, stupid research in his villa, living rich off stock holdings. At the time Griffin breaks in looking for sanctuary, he's busy writing a paper disproving invisibility! Another Eloi type, lax with inertia. How misfortunate it is upon Kemp that Griffin comes for aid. He needs a base for his Reign of Terror. Against villadom itself! So Kemp turns him in. Has to, rascal that he is. And then, poor Griffin is driven by dogs and police into town — where finally he is ringed and felled by navvies armed with spades. Dead, he turns visible, his magic betrayed.

JANE.   Who lives by the spade shall perish by the spade. Here, let **me** fix it.

LENIN.   (Takes off jacket).   Her housework is performed on my desk. Decodes all the mail from Russia. Copies all my letters, many copies to many comrades. In between, the lines in milk! Hot it over a candle to see. **That** is her cooking. She is bride of the revolution.

JANE.   She, too? Some revolution! (Exits).

LENIN.   A fine motto, **caveat vendor.** Agreed. But if Griffin is not shit-crazy like you say Doctor Moreau is not, why do you say, for example, this?   At end of novel, after Griffin hit to death with shovels, you say, "Thus ends the evil experiment of the Invisible Man."

HGW.   Irony again. Look for the opposite meaning. Failure is not failure.   It has rather the merit of negative experiments.   They set limits.   This won't do.   No way here. Revolution is just like science.   It progresses by a succession of experimental failures, each of which brings it nearer to success.

LENIN.   Your Griffin is not the first.

HGW.   No? Who?

LENIN.   Hmm. He is like Griffin, mad the same way, mad **at** things. He, this Russian hero, is not a criminal, as they say. Except maybe, he is a useful criminal. A bad person, not dainty to clean up shit–dirty world.

HGW.   Who is it?

LENIN.   It is a dark name.

HGW.   But tell me.

LENIN.   It is Nechayev. A name you do not know.

Lenin arrived in London on the 12th of April, 1902, and departed about a year later for Geneva, Switzerland. There he lived and pamphleteered and conspired until the eruptive events of 1917, in the midst of World War I, at which time he returned to Petrograd to lead the great October Revolution. Petrograd. Home and triumph for Herr Richter, LL.D. (a slight deception; he was not a Doctor but a Master of Laws). It had been St. Petersburg until named Petrograd in 1914 at the outset of the war, whose ruinous course for Russia, sliding down to organized defeat, he solicited, coming back to remodel a demodeled nation. Petrograd. Renamed Leningrad in 1924 upon the death of Lenin, secret Spade House pupil. Red-flagged Petrograd. Here the **bolsheviki** seized power for the total state, a Wellsian state-idea.

Lenin returned briefly to London during the summer of 1903 for a meeting of the Second Party Congress, where he first used the Lenin name in public and then did to Volgin in person what he did to his wallet portrait of Plekhanov in the presence of Wells. Tore him up. Ripped Volginism out of the movement. Reduced the founder and leader of the Social Democratic Labor Party and his Volginist followers to **mensheviki,** or "minoritarians." This was Lenin's downputting tag for the faction he outargued. His own he redefined as **bolsheviki,** or "majoritarian," majority being the

71

function of the conviction and superior shouting. The issue that split them was the revolutionary use of terror. **For** terror were the Bolsheviks. Under Lenin's leadership, they took Sergey Nechayev for their luminary and exemplar of the conspiratorial principle. The others, shunning that dread name — Nechayev — and his brazen rule, "the ends justify the means," found in him only the useless roguery of a scheming scoundrel. What had he done to be so misprized? Many things. At last, from the mute dungeons of the Alexis Revelin of the Peter and Paul Fortress, as "prisoner #5" he planned and directed the assassination of Tsar Alexander II. But for Lenin — how splendidly amoral this man! Like Griffin! With the Invisible Man for reminder, Lenin gained new respect for the revolutionary heritage of his native Russia. Who dares to say the Bolsheviks repudiate ethics and morality? Lenin now can answer, "Morality is that which serves to destroy the old exploiting society."

Nechayev is author of the sinister REVOLUTIONARY CATECHISM of 1869. One year later Jules Verne bodied forth its doctrine in the character of Capt. Nemo, hero of TWENTY THOUSAND LEAGUES UNDER THE SEA. Capt. Nemo, whose name means No-Name, is an alienated submariner with a cold passion for sinking British ships. An archangel of hate, he is a terrible judge of slave trading and colonialism. His no limit, selfless purpose is the star attribute of a Nechayev revolutionary. In the words of the CATECHISM, "He has no personal inclinations, no business affairs, no emotions, no attachments and no name." Lenin sees in Griffin's invisibility that namelessness, in his terrorism the boundless corrective. It is not madness, after all, but the moral grandeur of one strong with hatred, ready to tear himself away from the bonds which tie him to the social order with all its laws and petty habits of custom and tradition, and to endure complete withdrawal and solitude of purpose. Nechayev, like the Invisible Man, is above all an ethical revolutionary. "For him, morality is everything that contributes to the revolution. Immoral and criminal is everything that stands in the way." He despises everything about the existing order, above all the mundane sciences, leaving them to profit from the ruins and rebuild the future. "He knows only one science, the science of destruction. For this reason, and this reason only, he will study mechanics, physics, chemistry, and perhaps medicine." Not truth nor help, his one merciless object is "the prompt destruction of this filthy order."

HGW. But I **do** know him! Nechayev is one of my sources Jane doesn't know about.

LENIN.   I see why you are interested to learn Russian.

HGW.   His work of chastisement is my own.

LENIN.   Then there will be other Invisible Men? After Griffin?

HGW.   Griffin is Invisible Man the First. You follow.

LENIN.   A problem. He is, ah, uhm, too spontaneous with his feelings. No way to organize feelings of resentment.

HGW.   Isn't that rather the problem with Marxism?

LENIN.   I forgot.

HGW.   Any Morlock can burn barns. But **disciplined** terror —

LENIN.   — is for **professionals.**

HGW.   Like yourself. Stick with it. Remember what Griffin says to Kemp. "This is what we must do — not wanton killing, but a judicious slaying." Nothing spontaneous in a moral Reign of Terror **pour encourager les autres.** Nothing original there, you know the source: "Virtue without terror is powerless."

LENIN.   Robespierre!

HGW.   Through him the Great French Revolution achieved glory.

LENIN.   Kemp not listen.

HGW.   But you do.

LENIN.   He calls the police.

HGW.   Yes, and after Griffin had barely got started with a few broken windows and the unseen killing of one or two fools who crossed him. But never mind. We go on. There will be Invisible Man the Second, and so on, until the necessary clearance is done. Those dear old institutions!   The family, private property, patriotism, Christianity, trade unions, democracy.   Inept democracy!   Finally, his line will rule over the reconstruction to follow.   When the Napoleon of political organization we want shall come upon the scene, he will be our Invisible Great Man. He will be able to build without churchly or popular sanction. He will not be one of those rotten, rivalrous, partisan politicians, foolishly dependent on applause, wowing themselves into office by vote storms. He will avoid speechmaking and handshaking and all the fraud of seeking after public opinion.   Hence, the Great Man's invisibility. Why ask the Peepul, the swill of this brimming world, what they want? That is the error of democracy. We have first to think out what they **ought** to want if society is to be saved.

Then we tell them and we see that they get it. Our Invisible Great Man will build the state without the support of the crowd and even in spite of its dissent. His activities and whereabouts are mysterious, yet his unseen controls are **felt.**

For the hero-savior of the state, power is the key to popularity, not the reverse as in the democratic notion. Terror generates piety.

JANE.   (Enters with Lenin's coat).

LENIN.   You fixed it yourself?

JANE.   Who else?

LENIN.   Thank you. My apology, madam.

*

DATE LINE: Khabarovsk, U.S.S.R.

LETTER FIVE

Concerning THE WAR OF THE WORLDS (1898)

Stalin modern on huge display. No log-cabin villages anywhere near. Not like Nadhodka. This big-time urbanism. Khabarovsk. I go from here by Aeroflot to Moscow.

What is here, Moscow brought. Russian frontier. Used to be. So it was 1898. Year WAR OF THE WORLDS published, Lenin still in Shuskenskoya, next to last year of exile, Krupskaya joins him, marriage. They live in small cabin. Full of books. Translate HISTORY OF THE TRADE UNIONS by the two Webbs. Another darling couple. Useless project. So what? Lenin reads too fast. Not enough to do. Needs a state to run. When he does, trade unions are organs of government. Not free associations of Volginist type. Same with taming of frontier. Not filled up with self-acting migrants.   No Conestoga wagons ever came this way.   Only conscripts by rail.   Social duty to build war bases along Chinese border and on Pacific coast.   Part of Russian design for global federation of Soviet Republics.   Said Lenin, "Socialism is the United States of the World."   Lenin quoting Wells.   From last chapter, OUTLINE OF HISTORY.   Finished just before Kremlin visit 1920.   Title of chapter is, "The Next Stage in History."   End of the line.   Final stage is World Socialist State. Moscow time is planetary time.

Big buildings here are government offices.   Bureaus of the Politburo.   All offices in this unitary state the bureaus of its head bureau, the cephalic center in Moscow.   Gigantic piles of half columned marble, arrayed **en grande.**   Others are rat-house barracks in cast concrete, elongated for miles.   Frontier occupied per plan.   Home is wherever state assigns you one.   Not really home.   Just a functional address.   Efficient.   Labor force fluidized.   Moveable from area of surplus to area of need.   Just show your workpapers.   A welfare service, Minton would say.   No unemployment.   Right.   Jobs created by means of arrests. Welfare state is prison state.

The next lesson is held in the playroom of G.P. Wells, "Gip," the one-year old son. His father has already determined the course of floor games he shall follow as he grows up. This was considered in the design of Spade House. The home that has no floor upon which games may be played falls short of education. Accordingly, the nursery is paved with green-colored cork tiles without a pattern, which will take and show chalk marks and on which toy figures and such-like will stand up. Upon such a floor may be made many dreamy games, for the building up of spacious and inspiring political ideas for later life. In the coming world state, architecture is the master art. The toys to have are tin soldiers, citizen figures cast to HGW's order, a lot of clock-work railway rolling stock and rails, and immense quantities of custom carpentered bricks an inch thick or less, in sizes 18 X 9, 9 X 9, and 9 X 4, plus halves and quarters of these wholes, and some larger pieces of platform planking.

"Gip" is out with Jane for an afternoon airing, so Wells and Lenin have the nursery to themselves. HGW empties cartons of blocks onto the floor and begins building.

"I'll do London, you do Westminster. And don't forget the railway station. Or would you rather do Buda and Pesth?"

"London," says Lenin.

"The two parts of **Greater** London it is."

When they have built their twin cities across the carpet to the point of coalescence, they lay rails around and through it, with various switching points along the way. That done, HGW stands up, surveys the results, then with great pitch and moment, bends over and draws a chalk line between the ends of what is obviously one conurbation.

"Here is my mayor," he says, pulling a figure from the toybox.

"Where is mine?" asks Lenin, populating his part of town from the same box.

HGW scribbles a few stamp-sized posters, mounts them on toothpicks, and plants them on Lenin's side. They read, "Election Booth," "Vote for ME," and so forth. "Want to have an election?" he asks.

"Why for? You already have your mayor. I want mine."

"Two mayors? Two municipal boards? Must I negotiate with you to send my trains over there and back?"

As HGW queries in this manner, he winds up the locomotive and sends it down the line, pulling a string of wobbly goods cars. Lenin stops it with his hand.

"No mayor, no train. **He** decides if train comes here."

HGW gets up and, finishing the action, kicks the cars off the rails.

"So much for local patriotism. **That's** what your defense of it gets you, no train for Westminster, no social services at all. It's one mayor for Greater London, or chaos."

Lenin pulls futiley on the switches at his end.

"While you're at it, why not valve off your section of the water and sewage mains? Or cut off from the national power grid and generate your own electricity? Or run your own telephone service? Remember Richmond? Self-important places get left behind."

"Is Time Traveller's home borough," says Lenin. "What of it?"

"What **of** it?" No electricity!"

"Time machine . . . . But how . . . . His house, it is lit by gas jet, also kerosene lamps and candles."

"The time machine is a mechanical device," says HGW, picking up the toy engine and replacing it in the tracks. "It is in fact a bicycle mechanism, ridden on a saddle and pedalled, and the makers of bicycles are wonder workers. I ride mine on masterful adventures in and out and through any-which-ever tangle of little wards and vestries, and I meet and ride with unchaperoned girls on theirs. They are liberating machines. Soon they will develop into flying machines, and take us into the sky, and we shall look down and see no borders."

This is 1902. Even as Wells prophesies the advent of airplanes, the Wright brothers, two American bicycle mechanics, are building one and preparing to fly it.

"Then will all family, local and national entanglements be dissolved under the world rule of the coming engineers."

Standing up and looking down on the twin cities he and Lenin have built, he says, "All this and more will form but one Administrative Area under a World Council. So much for Richmond — and its mindless mayor."

"Ah," says Lenin.   "Time Traveller's guest, the skeptical one. Not believe in talk about time machine. Walks out on host when he hears that Time is only a kind of Space. He not like to hear that."

HGW picks up the engine and rolls its wheels on the palm of his hand. "Because the truth of it will **destroy** him — him and his petty parochial office. Time Travel, after all, comes to the same thing as the mastery of distance with rapid transport. Boundary lines are abolished. The same with **any** translocal public service, be it delivered by rail, pipe or wire. The mayor disdains time travel as he defends the right of Richmond borough to go against electricity.   Which he did, while others hooked into the London grid, or else were pleased to put in their **own** power stations. Or again, did nothing. Anything to keep the proud old places **theirs** to do the choosing. Decisions like this are being made everyday, right down to ward level, thanks to an Act of Parliament granting every last local authority its say about lighting, drainage, water supply, tramways, whatever. **And** schooling. And taxation, of course.   Every rural and district board, every parish and county council, borough and municipality. Treason! Treason against large-scale modernity. Well, Richmond's dwarfish space will have to be cleared away. As will **this.**"

Here HGW draws a long chalk line away from Greater London toward the direction of Surrey, and sketches in a number of irregular suburban communities. Shepperton, Weybridge, Addlestone, Chobham, Woking, Horsell, and the line is a commuter line marked, "London and Southwestern Railway."

Lenin suddenly gets the picture.

"Ah," he says. "Here is where the first three Martian boats land. Here, and here, and here."

He plunks down three blocks in Horsell, Woking and Addlestone, straddling the commuter line. "Shit localities given a blast of the Martain ray guns."

"And the others?"

Another three or four, I think. They land over here, in outer skirts of London, yah?"

Confirming, HGW places a group of four blocks on the edge of London and Westminster, and close by at Wimbledon and Bushey Park, next to Richmond, places which he names in chalk.

The two sit down on the green cork floor and HGW says, "And now you know the mission of the Martians."

LENIN.   The work of Siva. They destroy Vishnu of locality possession.

HGW.   More than that. Gigantic clearances followed by gigantic new constructions. Administrative areas demodeled and remodeled.

LENIN.   Dialectic at work, just so. Martian boats come down, three in Surrey, four in London area. They string out along London and Southwestern Railway tracks. Far from city center at one end, near it at the other. Pattern is this: two groups, they lie apart at longest distance of daily train ride. For people who ride to work.

HGW.   Exactly. All those commuters. Jobs in Metropolitan London, homes in Surrey. Yet it is only necessary that they **get** to work, not that they keep up their old fen and den culture out there. Surrey the county gave us the name for a four passenger carriage with a fringe on top, and our map is based on locomotion in the likes of it. The map is outdated. Horses and animal lairs for homes are no longer needed.

LENIN.   That is why the Martians blast home localities. Make room for bigger work community, yes?

HGW.   Go on.

LENIN.   Out of the boats, Martians raise up their walking tripods. Many houses high. Giant machines, walking over pygmy men. They move forth and back, fast like flying birds, you say. Moving so fast between landing places. And, each place, it is lit up at night by their big electric lights. The sky so bright where they are, it is a sign of big organization.

HGW.   Giants administering to sprawling urban growth, correct.   They are bigness insurgent, bigness organized. They plan to make a single unit of parts that used to be whole, but no longer can be, like suburban Horsell or Woking, resist the fact or not.   There can't be villages anymore, intact and ignorant as Iping is. The state monster that regulates all public service in future will suck the ebbing life from these little communities into the veins of the new, and swell its functional completeness.

LENIN.   Vampire talk you make.   That is why Martians eat human blood?

HGW.   Not eat, but yes. Having no digestive system, they pump it directly into their blood stream.

LENIN.   Like you, Marx hate shit-rural life.   His favorite place is London and British Library. Good riddance, Iping! Pigs for people. They not believe Invisible Man even when they see him, I mean, when they see his wonders. He is, how to say, too much **outside** them.

HGW.   Like Doctor Moreau, like the Martians, he is an incomprehensible, external force.

LENIN.   Yes, not easy to comprehend him. He waves chair at Mrs. Hall when he is not dressed, she rushes out, crowd gathers, they talk, even idea of invisibility comes up, but is pushed aside. Such a gathering — just like Parliament, a talking shop, no decisive action taken.

HGW.   Pigs is right. Or hole bolting rabbits, and not just in Iping. Its mental horizons extend no further than the ale house, and the same everywhere else. Men simply must unlearn the attraction and the necessity of home.   The den-dwelling, cave-comforting stage of human history, the littleness of it, is a thing that must go. A painful novelty it is the Martians teach, uprooting the human rabbit. For most people, not to have a return ticket is a disaster.   We can't expect human nature to give up cheerfully a familiar way of living in favor of social efficiency.

LENIN.   What means efficiency?   Man is not a machine.

HGW.   No, but society is, and the liberal idea does not serve it well.   The state needs to draft labor and move it anywhere the work community may require. That's the Martian idea.

LENIN.   Civilian army?

HGW.   Industrial army.   Compulsory service to a higher social order.

LENIN.   Conscript **civilians**?

HGW.   To organize for work is the primary duty of the state, and organization for work is socialism. Something more than the toy-town gas and water socialism of the Fabians. It is to municipalize **labor**. It's a new and untried thing, of course. Like changing one's language or emigrating to a land entirely foreign. Adjustment to the new necessities will be painful. For those willing to understand, however, our partymen will explain. They being men of intelligence without passion, they are unfeeling and unfailing political reasoners. Theirs is a new kind of state, the Education State. Teachers for rulers and pupils for citizens. And as for the unteachables, the dull who can't learn and the base who won't — well, people who cannot live in the new world without spoiling it for others are better out of it. Social efficiency means a new morality that makes killing worth the while; and like Abraham, the new Adam will have the **faith** to kill.

LENIN.   And the Martians. What are they to this?

HGW.   A prophecy, my good man, a prophecy. The Martians are advanced municipalizers. You saw that for yourself.

LENIN.   But they fail, Martians die. Defeated by, uh, bacterias. Dirty germs of Earth.

HGW.   Just another failed experiment. Defeated
merely by the gulf between their dreams and their power.   The
power will come. They show the way.

LENIN.   Ugly brutes. **Octopus** monsters!

HGW.   But nice monsters. Socialist monsters. Their
abode is a socialist planet. Mars is a dying world even as ours will
become. They do something about it. They start to leave and come
here. Do you suppose the failed remnants of humanity the Time
Traveller finds could do such a thing?   You know the work of
Percival Lowell, I assume.

LENIN.   Percival Lowell. American Astronomer,
telescope on mountain top in, I think, Arizona. His book, MARS, is
1895, same as your TIME MACHINE. He sees desert planet cross-
crissed with irrigation ditches, they bring water from melting hats
of polar ice. They go many thousands of miles, follow great circle
paths. Crossings make city places. Pattern of network is made by
one giant water authority. The order is Pythagorean. Geometry like
that is proof of rational beings.

HGW.   Proof of socialist correctness. Proof of large-
scale planning and ethical advance. The system is planet-wide, so
national politics have no part in them, so Lowell says. In this
abolition of political boundaries, under a world directorate, is to be

seen the direction of terrestrial progress.

LENIN.   Still, what can octopus teach to humans?

HGW.   A promising animal, the octopus. Think of its splendid eyesight, its suction-cup tentacles, its highly organized nervous system. No senses are more brainy than sight and touch. The Martians are octopodus monsters about the size of a bear, having a head four-feet in diameter, with two groups of eight tentacles growing from round the mouth.   They are dome-headed monsters of intellect.

LENIN.   No Martian seawater for them to come from.

HGW.   They don't come from the sea. They come from humanoids like ourselves. Somewhere there's a Doctor Moreau in their history. He must have done colectomies.

LENIN.   Huh?

HGW.   Evisceration. He must have taken out the intestines, and also removed the brain box, so as to allow the cerebral tissues to expand.

LENIN.   Great clumsy creatures.

HGW.   Not when at the controls of their tripedal walking engines a hundred feet high. Then they speed fast as birds, as you know. Anyway, the Martians are only a political metaphor.

A State Octopus is just the social invention missing in this world of ours, which has grown far too much muscle and stomach without nervous controls enlarged enough to manage it. The Martians are all brain and hands, avatars of Brahma the Creator, all knowing and making. Sleepless, sexless monsters they are, with no colon or genitals, no disharmony between thinking and feeling, no down time for indigestion or lust. The animal side of their nature has been dissected out. They are cool and unsympathetic, brain lords of tireless work. They are my prophecy of the coming beast, the State Octopus.

> LENIN. How they reproduce?

> HGW. Budding.

> LENIN. Very well. But they are not all Brahma. Their ray gun is a weapon of Siva.

> HGW. The Dialectic, man! You're forgetting it again. The Martian Heat Ray does the work of Siva **and** Brahma. It is a weapon **and** a tool, the instructional technology of the Education State.

> LENIN. How so? You cannot instruct dead people.

> HGW. The walking engines of the Martians — what do they walk on?

> LENIN. Three legs.

HGW.   And the one word I use?

LENIN.   Tripod.

HGW.   Now, then. What common device do you know that sits on a tripod?

LENIN.   Camera.

LENIN.   A photographic camera. The Martian tripods are camera tripods and the Heat Ray device is a camera, and is described as such in the novel.

LENIN.   But light beam comes **out** of Heat Ray box, does not go **into** box.

HGW.   What its eye looks upon, it zaps to pieces. Exactly what a photographic camera does! The Heat Ray is an item of Martian fighting equipment that makes war on tradition, so the future may come forth and be new. Creative destruction, the work of Brahma allied with Siva. That is the work of the photo industry, being done right now, and we must capture it for the revolution. Photographs destroy original art, and thereby diminish the intensity of the individual life. And what else but that is a precondition for the collective life?

LENIN.   It's just pictures, like paintings.

HGW.   How wrong you are. Look. Exposure to great original paintings is divisive and sectarian.   Each artist has his coterie of admirers. Not only in art museums. To buy a painting and hang it in the home is to have a taste for this over that, one painter or school of art over another. All art is invariably sectarian, even great cookery. The chef who cooks directly for a clientele that shares the earnest of his palate — it's a fashionable thing in London, Paris, New York, even your St. Petersburg.

LENIN.   I eat in cafes.

HGW.   You'd better notice this other. We have to see to it that it goes and gives way to food predigested in the social stomach. Canned food already points the way, the denatured stuff of mass chemical processing. We have only to bring it from factory to communal restaurants. So with the autotype, the photographic ditto.   What we want from **true** art, political art, is not private enthusiasm but the correct social function. What we want is mass admiration of the photo–duplicate, for intensification of the collective life. Autotypes, run off by the Educational State, will do just that, bring home a common visual stimulus.

LENIN.   Pictures of what?

HGW.   Above all, portraits of our Invisible Great Man — our program personified — who is not seen otherwise. Public appearances are for imposters, vote-swindling actors who play on the democratic illusion of preference and choice. Our first task is the disillusionment of self-reliance. If people think they can make private aesthetic decisions, they think as well they are capable of making moral and civic decisions on their own. But it's all individual and disconnected and quite socially irresponsible. Therefore, impoverishment of the sensual and aesthetic life, such as mass exposure to photo art, is basic to the **sharing** experience of socialism. The Martian Heat Ray is destructive in that creative way. The camera abolishes privacy.

LENIN.   Hmm, much thought in what you say. Your idea is, ah, most important, I'm afraid. It makes for me a new problem of the revolution, like problem Doctor Moreau has with beast people.

HGW.   How so?

LENIN.   Pain therapy not stick. Beast flesh creeps back.

HGW.   New experiments will improve on that.

LENIN.   I not mean lapsing of beast folk he makes. His method, as you say, can be better. But yet, you say also they have babies, but they are just animals.

HGW.   The human characteristics acquired by surgery in the House of Pain are not inherited, a problem I admit.

LENIN.   Well, it is not solvable. Offspring of beast folk are born again as beasts, not take on shape of laboratory parents. Next generation, and so on, must go back to House of Pain to get stamping on of human form. Work in House of Pain never finished. This is because your man-making is by external force, not natural.   In family and home town, babies grow up to be normal people. No trouble to make them so. To make them different, that is the problem.   If your Vampire State drains life-blood from community culture, then man has always to be manufactured, again and again, always.

HGW.   Of course. Men are born, citizens are made. Or rather **unmade:**   human tradition decultivated. The answer to your problem is to think in suns' distances. We have man's remotest futurity to consider. Yet it is all very simple. We have only to instruct people in the attachment of their labors to one great workshop of the world. That, and nothing more. The moment you have a local community or family ties, whenever you have Heart, you get the spirit of gain and the desire for property. We shall destroy that desire in its infancy, as it arises, though it be with us alway. Only the necessary is necessary, the spirit of service. Absolute service to mankind, absolute loss of individualtiy. That's for our elite of vocational terrorists to look after, confirmed in their duty forever. They must have the cosmic vision of the Time Traveller to see out the life cycle of the species to its most distant destiny. Suns may freeze and worlds may perish, but our purpose will never die, like the Martians we will find other worlds, travel across immensity to the stars, and when we have conquered all the deeps of space and all the mysteries of time, still we will be beginning.

Sitting there on the green cork floor, Wells waits a moment for effect, then abruptly demands, "Can you write backward?" With pencil he very rapidly writes three uneven lines on a little piece of play paper, and signs his name. Lenin gets to his feet and holds up the scribbly words to the nursery looking-glass, and reads,

our length

of will

is long

HG Wells

Not allowing Lenin to remain puzzled by the trick itself, Wells explains.

"I want you to understand that this is best done quickly. No weak, wishful velleities for the partyman."

Lenin's first act of seizure in the Revolution of 1917 was to take over the Petrograd telephone exchange. What he said into it is not recorded. The essential fact was his control of the network, Russia's nervous system.

Within the year of Lenin's final departure from London, in 1903, Wells joined the Fabian society, a group of tea-party socialists, the two Webbs presiding. Judging him on the political hints they found in the Scientific Romances, they invited him in, soon to get rid of him. His hints went far beyond the little projects of municipal jobbing they imagined to be the epitomy of socialism, town ownership of gas and water mains. Their study of trade unions, another Webby limitation, was the work Lenin took for misdirected effort to translate during his exile out there in Shushenskoya, only to find the stronger hints of H.G. Wells more to his liking, and by chance later met him at Spade House. But Wells himself failed to take the Fabian Society with the very same program Lenin had already accepted, and run off to Russia with in the name of Marx. A student of biology, Wells should have known better than to have tried it himself. With that squeaky voice and dumpy body of his, he had not the poise of the dominant mammal to pull off a political coup anywhere. Good he was with the passades and the young girls who liked his blue eyes and his diabetic body odor the smell of bee's honey, but the man couldn't run a dog fight, much less a party and a state. He remained the hidden theoretician to Lenin's open chairmanship.

The difference is, Lenin knew power comes first, theory next.

Only after Lenin took power did he reflect on it in Wellsian terms. With the advent of motion pictures, he instantly put the cinema to work in making propoganda films, forceful films, as we know. This was only to be expected, as were the ubiquitous Lenin portraits, the execution cellars and the corrective labor camps. But what he finally **said** about education and re-education founded the principle of long perspectives in effect to this day. He established this policy of statism taught him in the Spade House nursery:

Each new revolutionary generation must learn the lesson of the Revolution all over again.

LETTER SIX

Concerning THE FIRST MEN IN THE MOON (1901)

Once again, Moscow.   Home of Socialist Central Time.   Back to Hotel Ukraina.   Without Minton.   Thank God. Thanks for what?   Tomorrow, Lenin Library.   Find letter.   **Find** it.   Or get caught searching.   Where hidden?   My hunch . . . . If wrong?   Meanwhile I take dinner.   Not in hotel dining room. Not where Minton and I used to.   Drat the man!

I go outside.   Visit nearby cafeteria.   Eating place for natives.   Foreigners not come here.   This the real thing.   No napkins.   Run on statist lines.   Even cabbage soup served up the Wellsian way.   Heritage of Leninism.   Here's how.   Three ladies in white smocks.   Wearing funny hospital hats.   Public health agents.   Witches of the sanitary utopia, disinfected of moral self-action.   Standing over three kettles, in a row.   I move bowl on

tray along guide rails.   One dips up broth.   One the cabbage

leaves.   One the bits of meat.   A fourth supervises.   Valuable

ingredients.   Can't be trusted to one person.   Not like American

sales girl, running store counter all by herself.   Show goods, make

sale, wrap up, take money, do everything.   Terribly self-reliant.

Awfully self-sufficient.   Balefully bourgeois.   Inner-directed.

Can't have this here.   New proletarian ethic means workers not

trusted.   Honesty a selfish personal virtue.   Comes the higher

morality of socialism.   No more individual motives.   Organization

is   e*x*t*e*r*n*a*l   substitute   for   responsibility.

D+I+V+I+S+I+O+N   O+F   L+A+B+O+R   U+N+D+E+R

L+E+A+D+E+R+S+H+I+P   O+F   A   C+E+N+T+E+R.   Cabbage

soup statism.   Man's conquest of the social order.   The way it's

done in the moon.   Lenin learns this last day at Spade House.

          It is Sunday afternoon. In a few hours Lenin will catch

his train for London.   Soon after he will travel to Geneva, then

Zurich, later to Petrograd and the Revolution, and thence to

Moscow.   From his Kremlin office there, the Chairman of

Sovnarkam will put into action not Marxism, but the Spade House

Dialectic. Meanwhile, he and Wells take a stroll around the house, walking off their big Sunday dinner.

Looking up at the house as they circle it, Lenin is curious to know which aspects, other than the floor plan, Wells himself designed. Not much else, Wells explains. Those unionized craftsmen! Their construction methods, strictly Medieval. He wanted poured concrete, and they refused. Better, he would have wall squeezed out as one squeezes toothpaste from a tube. Instead, he had to watch his walls go up brick by brick, listen to the tinkling trowels, every mason joining brick to mortar, one by one in wasteful repetition of each other's work.

LENIN.   Yes, it is a great question considered by Marx.

HGW.   House construction?

LENIN.   Society.

HGW.   How so?

LENIN.   Your brick layers. Marx agrees. Their bad method of work is method of capitalist society.

HGW.   Is that so? And how does **Marx** find fault with them?

LENIN.   It is with their division of labor.

HGW.   Nonsense. The mason is a specialist, a craft specialist.

LENIN.   It is in Marx. To him, division of labor and private property, they are cause and effect. The work makes the result.

HGW.   As usual, he's all mixed up.

LENIN.   Listen. There is physical work and there is mental work. There are factory workers, all day with their hands. Then there are factory owners. Morlocks and Eloi, yes? Also shit politicians, fancy intellectuals and writers. **More** Eloi. Not you, excuse please. Do they use brain life to help Morlocks? Do Morlocks enjoy Eloi leisure? This is division of labor Marx means. Lazy class on top, toils on bottom. Destroy this, and we destroy capitalism.

HGW.   Private property will of course have to go. The possessions of Vishnu. All men will be equal when they are equally propertyless and equally dependent on the all-property-owning state. The question is, who will disendow them? It will take a new class better than any seen before. A revolt of labor will not raise it.

LENIN.   What you say is garbage! Under socialism, factory workers have abilities to accomplish anything.

HGW.   Who will **give** them socialism? We've come so far, yet Volginism you love all the same. Worker fulfillment! The socialist state is not a hospital charity. It is a machine for making progress, without do-nothing Eloi or dully industrious Morlocks getting in the way.

LENIN.   Look, I show you. (Pulls out notebook full of quotations from Marx, and quickly flips through it to the citation he wants). Here. He says, under capitalism each man has a life of work to do. He is, uh, let me translate. He is a hunter. A fisherman. A shepherd. A critical critic. And so on, and he must do this one work or he does not eat. Exploitation!

HGW.   How bucolic for a man of the study.

LENIN.   Not just out-of-doors work. There is the shepherd but also the critic. Marx wants physical and mental to be in one person. More healthy that way, not capitalist way.

HGW.   But the occupations you mention are not examples of subdivided labor, which is, by the bye, quite the essence of the coming state.

LENIN.   It is here! (Stabs notebook with finger).

HGW.   The usual confusion between division of labor and specialization, as I have said. Stubborn you are.

LENIN.   I go on. Then Marx gives the future. Under socialism I will be able to hunt in the morning. Fish in the afternoon. Rear cattle in the evening. Criticize after dinner. Without ever do I have to become hunter, fisherman, shepherd or critic. Dream of Marx is undivided man.

HGW.   Men are that already and too much. I repeat, division of labor is not the same thing as to **specialize** in a self-serving personal economy. In future, only the state will have an economy. Would you destroy what we must have if we are to have socialism?

LENIN.   Cooperation?

HGW.   A wronger word I do not know. Cooperation! The piety of every errorist that ever was. Sheer barter, a trade in help and mutual service. Socialism, dammit, is not people working for other people, it is people working for the state. We need do less with the spirit of the artisan and more with that of the soldier. We want mankind **drilled.**   Duty, discipline, direct public service. Selfless work, done by the individual without the -ism. Unpaid work anybody can do, people atomized without false regard for cultivated habits of craftsmanship and personal autonomy.

LENIN.   So we shall make a small grammatical change in Marx. Then it still is possible for me to hunt in the morning, fish in the —

106

HGW.   Stop! This is idiocy. You're not listening. We can't let men run **loose** anymore.   What you get with Marx is a collective nothing.   Total lack of organization.   No coordinated work.   It's premodern, it is medieval, it is totally piecemeal, it is the worker being **himself** in his work, cobbling away at his personal artifact, the shoemaker making shoes in his one-man workshop, the watchmaker his benchmade watch, the potter his oven batches of pottery, your cowboys and anglers, those **masons** of mine, brick after brick . . . .   My god, the pyramids were built that way!   But someday, I tell you, things will be different.   Things will **flow.** Houses built, one man to operate a wall-squeezing machine, another to form its surface with a pat or two.   No more batch work. Continuous flow production. Industry reinvented.

What have we now for factories?   Mere agglomerations of craftsmen, a cluster of ateliers under a single roof.   Cottage industry is all, huger and formless.   There is no organic unity in this, no flow process, only wasteful repetition.   Someday the industrial worker will be taken out of himself to become an object of truly functional utility, part of a world economic machine, governed by a single directive intelligence.   He will be despecialized, deindividualized, a corpuscle in the collective body of the New Leviathan. His individual self will flow into the common self, and merge with its great design. And **that,** my dear sir, is what specialization is not. It is a division of tasks linking all men completely together in the execution of a creative plan, activating all human assets and directing them towards one common purpose. On this basis will the future efficiency of industry rest, and be a model for social management and a new moral world.[*]

LENIN. Like the way it's done in the moon?

HGW. Yes, yes, yes!

LENIN. Well, I thought moon society of Selenites is just political model, not industrial as well.

HGW. It is all of that, and more. State and society are one. Just what **did** you see in it?

LENIN. FIRST MEN IN THE MOON is 1901, when it gives me new idea how to run SD Party. So, I write WHAT IS TO BE DONE? Published last month before I come here. This will make trouble for Volgin swine and other editors of ISKRA. They think newspaper is for news. What to do is turn it around, make news-

---

[*] Editor's note. This prophecy was made in 1902, six years before the advent of the assembly line, pioneered in 1908 by Henry Ford for the mass production of Model T automobiles.

paper in reverse: information in, orders out. Editorial board to be Central Committee, executive center of Party, then Party is underground government, ready to take over when guns of revolution shoot. Party organized like small, secret army, sending little detachments here and there all over Russia, with command center in newspaper office. ISKRA not print news only. Paper is organ to unify policy for all comrades, send orders, hear replies.

HGW.   Go on. In what way was the novel helpful?

LENIN.   What I like is your Grand Lunar. He is vast, jelly-shaking brain who runs the moon. Brain is many yards in diameter. His mental arms are long. All Selenites are his extra hands.

HGW.   Tentacles.

LENIN.   He is, what you say, Napoleon of political organization. All Selenites do his bidding in every cavern of the moon. Exist only to obey his orders, the duties they have to perform. I say to myself, this is how to organize Party, find place for all revolutionaries in Party cells back home. No questions, just do, report back to Party headquarters in ISKRA office.

But one thing I want to know. What kind of insects are

your Selenites? You say moon is one super ant-hill, but they are not ants, they are part insect, part vertebrate. That is contradiction.

HGW.   Not at all. They are **artificial** ants. Human souls molded in the imitation of insect bodies.

LENIN.   Yet there are so many types ... like in real ant nest which has worker, soldier, male with wings, queen and slave.

HGW.   Hundreds of types in fact, all of them produced by the educational methods of Doctor Moreau. Social surgery. The lunar House of Pain adapts each one of them to the social need he meets. Workers are all hands, messengers just spidery legs, instructors are trumpet faces, bladder brains for executive officers. The rest of each, except for his organ of purpose, is allowed to grow only enough to keep alive this essential part of him. His life is the exercise of his function. And so he attains his end, as dictated by the Grand Lunar. Division of labor under leadership of a center. Each Selenite, of whatever condition, is a perfect unit in a world machine. In the moon, every citizen knows his place.

LENIN.   Citizens? **World** machine? Moon is not just a militant pattern for Party machine?

HGW.   Can't you see? The Party has to be a model for society as well. The type of training and discipline our partymen put on themselves to-day, they will have to impose on the whole world to-morrow. They must pledge to that or what is revolution for? A single terrestrial ant-hill is the only way to save the human future. The moon is a replica of universal order.

LENIN.   This is not Marxist revolution. Marx is concerned to want a blending of physical and mental exercise for healthy growth of all human beings. Your moon workers are only hands, your moon executives only their brains. They are partial people.

HGW.   Completed in the Grand Lunar. He links together the whole varied body of labor in one united host. In **him** is affirmed your ideal — and mine — that of seeing to a common bond between intellectual workers and those workers who labor with their hands. Marx is too humanitarian, his fallacy. He would unite mental and physical assets in the individual by way of self-culture.   For him, the socialist morality of duty and service is a private morality, volunteered. But how bank up personal virtue? Redistribute it for the common good? Impossible. Only duties without honor can be distributed. Each individual can never be perfect but humanity can be, and all will share in **its** perfection. In the moon, there is no such thing as a complete person, only categories of utility. If the object in view is to realize a collective form of man, this presupposes a hierarchy of parts. Each part is perfect when it is all that it can be and does well all that it ought to do, a tentacle of the State Octopus. The state monster is the one and only unit of social life, the smallest as well as the largest. And the legend of Leviathan is, Division of Labor under Leadership of a Center. Only the aggregate is everything, one organism, one purpose. One integrated workshop. Its brain life is the directive intelligence of the front office, its physical life the factory hands. The co-partnery of brain and hands has its being in the Grand Lunar through his external tentacles. He **is** that State Octopus and the very embodiment of the Spade House Dialectic.

LENIN.   He is ruler for life. Like Plato's king bee, yes?

HGW.   You have an objection from Marx?

LENIN.   He does not consider rulership at all, I fear. A big mistake for the revolution. Yet it must be considered. The Party must have its head, the Central Committee. And after the revolution, the Party brain cannot stop working. So I think you maybe tell me more. How, in practice, you make Spade House Dialectic to govern the moon?

Wells invites Lenin to sit down at a garden table, takes his notebook from him, turns to a blank page, and graphs the following under a magic heading that promises to explain everything.

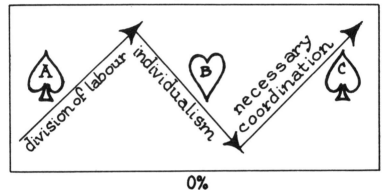

UNIVERSAL DIAGRAM

113

HGW.   Here's how it works. Letter "A" is the external force of Siva, the moving spirit of despecialization. This first arrow going up shows Him assigning more and more impersonal duties. That done all the way, a division of labor carried out one hundred percent, then Vishnu at letter "B," the spirit of individual motive, is denatured and reduced to zero percent. The arrow coming down is Her animal ego in decline, a measure of the resulting loss of self-action. As it hits bottom, the loss is total. And behold! Brahma the Creator, the letter "C," emerges and culminates. He is the spirit of coordination, and with His percentage rising to the full, making interdependence a necessary condition of life, here at the top of this last arrow, socialism is builded.

When the State Octopus is thus animated by a common creative impulse, the individual is at once most useful to society and least fit to live on his own. Unable to be self-reliant, the worker-citizen has no choice but to give himself to public service, it is inevitable. Not responsible for initiative, his reliability is absolute. It is the outcome of a rigid play of events, originating at letter "A" by Siva the Terror. To social-ize is to atomize.

On the eve of his departure from Zurich to Petrograd, Lenin wrote in STATE AND REVOLUTION (1917) his most famous line revising Marx, foretelling the industrial principle of cabbage soup statism he intended to effect on taking power.

> The whole of society will have become a single office and a single factory.

EDITOR'S ENVOI

We have a seventh letter from Tersoff, actually an eighth as well, this last a short note mailed for him from parts unknown in the Caucasus by his captors. It asks that none be published. The seventh we hold back, the least we can do for him, but the others we have gone ahead with, the most we can and should do for the public's right to know what can be known of the Minton Affair. After all, he did ask his attorney from the first to release his letters if he didn't come back.

His captors were not KGB. As he came out of the Lenin Library, stepping down onto the street, he was instantly run to ground by a huge gravel truck displaying a portrait of Stalin on the windshield. We can imagine his double fright, at first gasp thinking himself captured by one force, and then knowing it was by another. Scooped up by the seat mate of the driver, and forced into the cabin, he discovered the image of Stalin was not what he thought it to be. Not a banner of terror and tyranny imposed from above, but one of freedom raised up by young workingmen from below. Not old enough to remember the really bad old days, these truckers are far from nostalgic for Stalinism. Rather they are rebels in the only cause they know, their own liberty, and they have made it Russia's cause as well. Showing the Generalissimo's image, they protest the current leadership and the senselessness of life today under it. Grotesque and inappropriate as his mustachioed face may be, every portrait of Stalin on a trucker's windshield is a **no**! to the reigning Number One's portrait. It is a warning sign, like the red arrow on a motor vehicle's heat gauge, that says things cannot go on this way. Something has to change. And when it does, it will not be to the advantage of Stalin. Or Lenin. Or Wells.

Did he find the letter? Yes, that he did. It was not interleaved in the collected works of Lenin, as he had supposed, and he sat there a long while at his table in the Scholar's Reading Room on the second floor, looking out the lengthy row of high windows facing the Moscow River. What to do now? He was a little surprised that the reading room had not been closed, until he realized the official search had been and still was going on quietly. He noticed the two browsers going through the bound volumes of PRAVDA seated in shelves under the windows, thoroughly examining them from both ends. Then he knew. Of course. The day Wells visited Lenin back in early October of 1920. PRAVDA would have reported it. But the plainclothesmen were closing in on that year. With no time to lose, he got up, went over to the right volume, found the right issue, and there it was! He took the volume to his table, slid the letter into his notebook, and tried to look busy scribbling before making a too hasty departure. When the KGB officers reached the gap, they went over to the head librarian's desk to get permission to disturb a reader. Such unusual respect for the old book culture! That was his cue to get up and go, letter slyly slipped into his pocket. Not even his notebook was inspected. An oversight?

The KGB draws its officers from the cream of university students, and some of them have learned to think for themselves. One of them, from somewhere in the ranks, was in touch with that truckdriver, keeping him informed of Tersoff's whereabouts. "My Dear Wells" is now the prize of Rebel Russia. Captured by its agents as he walked out, he joined them, and is now a political philosopher in the Volginist undergound. Or do you say Menshevik?

Someday that letter will be published, and then we shall see what that portends. But these others are our business here.

end